Hey,
Dad!

Also by Brian Doyle

Hey, Dad!

Brian Doyle

Groundwood Books

© Brian Doyle 1978
All rights reserved.

First mass market edition 1991

Groundwood Books /
Douglas & McIntyre Ltd.
585 Bloor Street West
Toronto, Ontario
M6G 1K5

Canadian Cataloguing in
Publication Data is available

ISBN 0-88899-148-7

To Georgie and Peter

This is the story of how I hated my Dad for a while for some reason and how I loved him again for some reason and how I almost ruined a trip my family took to the Pacific Ocean and how all of a sudden I got independent for a while that summer when I was thirteen.

1

We were going to drive from Ottawa, where I live, to the Pacific Ocean. Mum and Dad had been planning the trip for months. It was going to be the biggest thing that ever happened to us.

There was only one problem.

I didn't want to go.

I was President of our "Down With Boys" club and the headquarters was in the old coal bin at my place and we were in the middle of fixing it up with a desk and curtains and stuff, so why should I have to leave it all just to go on some trip?

Where was the club going to hold meetings when I was gone?

The summer was going along just fine, so why ruin it?

All my friends told me that on any car trip they ever took all that ever happened was that they were car-sick. One of my friends told me that her family drove from Ottawa all the way to Halifax and she was sick out the window or in the ditch sixty-three times. She said she knew it was sixty-three times because she kept count by putting a little scratch on the ash-tray with her nailfile every five times she was sick. There were twelve scratches on the ashtray and she was getting ready to add another one when she got to Halifax. She said she read in a book that people in prison used to count the days that way by putting marks on the walls of their prison cells.

So she might as well have been in prison!

Once, our neighbours across the street tried to go on a big car trip to Arizona. The family spent about two weeks packing and on the last day they loaded their old car down with tons of stuff on the top and in the back and they all piled in and the neighbours were out waving goodbye to them and they took off.

About five minutes later, with all the neighbours still standing around the street talking about the trip, who should come around the corner but the travellers with smoke pouring out of the car and everybody hanging out the windows.

They never did go to Arizona.

They were lucky to get around the block.

I told these things to Dad while we were taking our sleeping bags to get drycleaned.

He looked at me for a while.

"We're going anyway," he said.

And that was that.

And I guess that's when I started doing what Mum calls a "slow burn".

It began with the pasting the map incident.

Don't tell me that everyone pastes a map to the inside of the car on the ceiling every time they decide to take a trip. I asked everybody and I couldn't find a single one who had pasted a map to the ceiling of their car.

Of course, Dad told us that *everybody* did that.

So my brother Ryan and I got the big map of Canada and cut the margins off to make it fit. Dad said to be sure and paste it facing west. It took us a long time to figure out which way was west because our car was in the laneway at the time. So I'm standing there like a dummy with the map. I'm turning it over and looking up and trying to figure out which way west is.

"If we are travelling west, which is what we plan to do, which way will the front of the car be facing? West, of course. So paste the map so that Vancouver Island is closest to the front of the car and you'll have it right," Dad says.

Mum said that the map was really a good idea because we would learn a lot about the geography of Canada that way and also it might give us something to do so that Ryan's fighting and mine would be kept down to a "civilized level".

Anyway, Ryan and I were in the back of the small station wagon on a beautiful sunny Sunday near the end of July figuring out how to paste the map on the ceiling when Dad and Mum came out to help.

Dad said that somebody should lie in the back of the wagon with the seat down and try to judge exactly where to place the map.

"See dummy," Ryan said. "That's what I said!"

I hit him really hard and I didn't even care when he cried for nineteen minutes.

Then Dad and Mum both lay in the back of the wagon on their backs and decided where to place the map. They were both laughing and talking and whispering and I felt like crying. I guess I wished I were as old as they were because it seemed like so much fun to be that old. When you're a kid you can never find anything to do.

Our next job was to get the suitcases strapped inside the rack on the roof of the car. Dad had a big elastic thing with seven legs called a spider that stretched over the cases and hooked on each side of the rack. Then Mum brought out three huge plastic bags with pull-strings that she sewed out of sheets of plastic we had in the cellar and we slid the cases inside each bag.

Rosy and Guildy were playing in the bags while we were working. Rosy and Guildy are two cats. Their names are short for Rosencrantz and Guildenstern, two funny characters in Shakespeare's play, *Hamlet.* Dad named our cats that. The only trouble was, Rosencrantz and Guildenstern in the play were both males and our cats are male and female. Dad said that was alright because in the play those two guys couldn't figure themselves out half the time anyway. Mum laughed a little bit when he said that and Ryan burst into fits of laughter, why I don't know. I didn't get the joke, so I couldn't see how *he* would get it. Ryan still laughs at everything Dad says whether he gets it or not. Anyway, Mum and Dad were giggling in the back of the car, and Rosy and Guildy were playing around too and Ryan was racing around being Ryan and I was just standing there feeling mad and alone and kind of empty.

By Sunday evening we had the car packed. We had

a cooler full of ice and food (pickled eggs, butter, ham, lettuce and stuff like that), a hibachi and some charcoal, a covered box for dry food (bread, peanut butter, onions, potatoes), and an open box (a bread board, cutlery, pots and stuff). On the top we had the three suitcases in their plastic bags, strapped down. The rest of our baggage was just ourselves. Oh yes, we had two extra handbags in the back seat for bathing suits, extra sweaters, towels and things.

We were ready.

All we had to do now was wait until early the next morning to start our trip.

Mum laid out all our clothes for the morning and made us go to bed in our underwear because all our pyjamas were packed and she wanted to start out with a "clean slate". My jeans and top and socks and shoes were on the chair beside my bed just the way they would be if I had been inside them sitting in the chair myself. The light from the hallway shone in my half open door onto the chair and I lay there looking at the clothes.

I could hear Mum and Dad talking about leaving the key with our neighbour next door so that she could come in and feed Rosy and Guildy.

Then I heard a little cat noise at my window and Rosy and Guildy came in their private entrance up the cedar tree and Guildy cuddled up beside my chin and started his motor. Rosy jumped off the bed with a furry thud and made a right turn into Ryan's room.

I spoke into Guildy's ear in a loud whisper.

"I'm *not* going," I said.

Guildy's ear bent down flat and he shook his head.
I shouted a whisper into the other ear.

I said, "I'm *not* going!"

He got up and went down to the other end of the bed.

We got up at five o'clock and we were on our way at half past. I woke up (really woke up) about six. The car was purring up Highway 17, soft and furry, through the fog. We were on our way.

All the way to Golden Lake, Dad was giving us this big talk on restaurants. We were never going into a restaurant from one end of our trip to the other. We had the hibachi, we had the cooler and the food and we were going to eat at picnic tables all across Canada. Restaurant food wasn't nearly as good as food you cooked yourself outside where everybody pitched in like a family team. When everybody helped with the food it tasted better and it was better for you. Also, it was better to be in the outdoors, in the countryside. You'd see more and get a better idea of what Canada was really like. You'd get to talk to other travellers, picnickers and campers on the way and you'd get a feel for each province as you went. It would be *educational*! And the money. Look at the money we'd save! Instead of giving a whole lot of our money to strangers we could spend it on ourselves when we saw things we wanted.

Then we turned into a restaurant in Golden Lake and ate a whole mess of bacon and eggs for breakfast.

After breakfast we headed for Algonquin Park. Canada didn't look very big at all. It was pouring rain and half dark because of the clouds and we could only see as far as the red brake lights of the car ahead of us. When we turned at Eganville, Ryan was naming the types of cars that we saw on the road, but I was thinking about where I had heard the name Eganville before. Then I knew. A boy in my class two years ago had moved from Eganville to Ottawa, and only lasted about two weeks. He was killed by a car just outside the gate of our schoolyard.

Then I started worrying.

I can still ruin more good times when I start to worry. Ryan is lucky. He never seems to worry.

Algonquin Park. I was expecting a lot from Algonquin Park. Maybe it was TV or what my teachers said or just the sound of the name Algonquin, but I couldn't wait to see Indians in the bushes and fantastic wild woods and rushing streams and growling bears and shy deer by the roadside. All I saw was the gate we went through with the sign about firearms. The man at the gate asked us about guns. Dad had a little laugh in his voice when he said no, we had no guns with us. It's a little laugh that comes inside the words sometimes when he's really saying, "What do you take me for, somebody stupid or something?" When he uses that laugh on me I don't like it at all. But when he uses it on somebody else I get a kind of chill on the back of my neck because I know what he really means.

We drove all the way through Algonquin Park. I saw bush on both sides of the road for the whole drive. Bush and rain. No Indians of course, and no animals.

"Algonquin Park!" I said. "Big deal!"

It was still raining. Ryan and I put the seat down and lay down in the back on our stomachs and looked at each other....I was looking right into his eyes. His eyes are big and a deep blue colour. I had a feeling that I liked him. It was a funny feeling. A kind of pain in the stomach. I silently vowed I would never fight with him again.

When I woke up the car was stopped. We were in Parry Sound. The sun was out. Dad was in the beer store. I mentioned, rubbing my eyes, that Dad was in the beer store.

"That's what I just said, dummy," Ryan said.

I hit him as hard as I could.

In half an hour we were through Parry Sound and we were stopped at a picnic table beside a small lake and we were having the first of our many outdoor meals.

Dad made the sandwiches and opened the drinks. Ryan caught a pollywog and Mum and I soaked the sunshine up. Whenever Mum and I get out of a car or come out of a door of a house or a store we always look up to see where the sun is. Then we look around to see where *we* are. If we're getting gas, for instance, Mum and I have our backs on the car and our faces up to the sun. We start doing this about the end of March and we're still doing it in early November just before the winter comes down on us like a big blanket.

So it was sunshine and sandwiches in Parry Sound.

Later Dad was talking to two kids around my age standing by the water skipping stones. I thought for a minute he knew them but when I asked him he said no.

"Then why were you talking to them?"

"I was asking the boy where he learned to skip stones, and I asked the girl why she didn't skip stones and did she think that skipping stones was just a sport for boys only, and then I asked the girl if she would pick up a pollywog, and then I asked the boy if he ever ate a live pollywog and then I told them that that's what we had for our lunch; live pollywog sandwiches with mayonnaise and then we went on to discuss the pollution situation and the problems in the Middle East and then ... "

"Forget it. Let's get in the car and get this trip over with. How far is this Pacific Ocean, anyway?"

Mum had her maps out and announced we were on our way to the moon when I remembered the map on the ceiling. The map. Look at the map and see how far we've gone! Ryan and I put the seat down and lay on our backs. Only that little bit! You mean to say that that's *all* the ground we've covered? It's not even an inch! Look! From Ottawa to Parry Sound is only about an inch!

"We drove all this way and we only made an inch."

"Hey, Dad," Ryan said, "we only came an inch!"

My heart sank. This was going to take forever!

"The map is about three feet wide and we've only covered one inch of it," I said.

"Will you cheer up?" Dad said.

"Next stop, the moon," Mum said.

"What do you mean, the moon?"

"Wait till we get to Sudbury," Mum said, "and you'll see."

Mum was right.

Sudbury *is* the moon.

All the way up to Sudbury we listened to Roberta Flack. We heard her about twelve times singing the same song because we kept switching stations. Everything was quiet except for the wind blowing in Dad's window and Mum humming a little bit.

I like when Mum sings along with the radio. She doesn't ruin the song she's singing along with like most people do. She leaves out the high notes and the low notes and just hums or sings the in-between ones. She just does the ones that she's sure of, I guess. She's very considerate that way. Why should everybody listen to a bunch of notes you can't even sing? So Mum was just chiming in with the notes she was good at. Ryan was having an afternoon nap.

And old Roberta was singing.

> *oooo*
> *That's the time*
> *Ah feel like makin' luh-huv to you;*
> *mmmmmmmmmmmmmmmm'*
> *That's the time,*
> *Ah feel like makin' dreeeeeeeeems come true!*

I was leaning with my chin resting in between the two front bucket seats and letting the vibrations rattle my teeth a little to the music. Dad was switching stations and Mum was keeping track of the map and naming the towns as they went by. Point au Baril Station, Byng Inlet, Bigwood, Estaire.

Speeding up the road, switching stations, looking for Roberta.

> *Ohhh, babe!*
> *In a restaurant*
> *Holdin' hands by candlelight . . .*

Funny how songs can remind you of things that happened a long time ago. Songs are the best things of all for reminding you of stuff. And smells too. One time a man came over to our place and sat in the kitchen smoking his pipe. The smell of his pipe reminded me exactly of my grandfather who died. I could almost see Grandpa sitting there in the kitchen if I let my eyes go half shut.

> *When you're touchin' me,*
> *And my feeling starts to show . . .*
> *ohhh . . .*

Those words can make me feel like I am right there in the car going to Sudbury all over again. The song makes me feel funny and I get a little red in the face and I get a little tight scared feeling in my stomach.

Dad said that he got a feeling when they played the song that they used to play when he would take Mum to dances before they were married and I asked him what the name of it was and he said he couldn't remember it at all, and then he started to laugh and fool around the radio looking for more Roberta, and Mum started hitting him, not too hard, on the shoulder with her map, and he started singing in a real loud awful voice some song about "the pale moon" or something. And Mum added some of the words and they were really laughing hard.

> Walkin' in the dark,
> Seein' lovers do their thing,
> ooo,
> ooo,
> That's the time,
> Ah feel like makin' luh-huv to you . . .

Then, suddenly, we could see it up ahead of us. Not a tree, not a bush, not a leaf. Just bare, ugly-coloured rock for miles and miles. Walter Cronkite never told us that the moon was just north of Parry Sound. But this was uglier than the moon. Dad pulled the car off the road. Ryan woke up and said he had to go to the toilet. There was no breeze and the sun was hot and there was a funny smell in the air. Dad was opening the back of the car. We were going to have a little snack.

"Where?"

"Up there."

Up there was hot rock and stink.

"Why?" I said.

"It's educational."

"I think it's horrible!"

"Who asked you?" Dad said.

Dad had pickled eggs, buns, two beers and two Cokes in a small box. When he gets his mind made up about something, he doesn't even ask. He just starts out and you have to follow.

We followed in single file up the smelly rock.

We were up the slope looking down on the car, the highway, and miles and miles of ugly nothing. I could have been on "Star Trek". Ryan skinned his knee and cried a bit. We were all tired and hot.

We caught up to Dad. He was squatting on the rock opening the drinks.

"How pastoral," Mum said.

"It's educational," Dad said again.

We started on the buns and Cokes and beer.

"All this is caused by years and years of mining and smelting and the fumes killed all the vegetation ..."

"I hate it here," I said.

"Me too," Ryan said.

"So pastoral," Mum said.

"It's EDUCATIONAL," Dad said.

Then I said it. I opened my mouth.

"You can *keep* your education!" I said.

And that started it.

He looked at me. He was mad. I could tell because when he gets mad he stares right at you and he swallows and his apple moves up and down his neck like it's trying to come up into his mouth. He stood up.

21

He was still staring at me. His shadow went way across the slope. He was between me and the sun. He had a pickled egg in one hand and a bun in the other. He raised his pickled egg hand, leaned back sort of like a baseball player and heaved the egg high in the air.

It sailed over my head in a big arc. I almost fell over backwards trying to watch it go down and disappear over the sloping rock.

There wasn't a sound. When you throw a pickled egg on the moon, it doesn't make any noise.

Then he turned around and walked with big steps down toward the car. The bun dropped out of his other hand and bounced down the stinking rock.

By the time we got the stuff picked up and caught up to him he had the car running. We got in and nobody said a word.

We drove through the bare rock.

I hated that place.

I hated this trip.

I hated Dad.

The whole time we were looking for a place to stay for the night, Ryan kept talking about the big nickel we saw in Sudbury. Nobody was saying a word except Ryan talking about the nickel. A big statue of a nickel.

"I'll give you a dime if you forget that nickel."

Nobody laughed.

Usually my jokes go over pretty well but this time all I got was silence. One of the quietest times in the world is after a lousy joke.

2

We finally found some cabins past Sudbury, near Nairn, called the Wagonwheel. It was a cute little place, all brightly painted red and white with a whole lot of knick-knacks on the front lawn and a pair of picnic tables. Could we swim anywhere around here? Yes, the lady who ran the place told us, there was a little river just across the highway and down the path.

Down the path under the trees it got cooler and cooler and then we heard the water gurgling. Me first, then Ryan. Then Dad. Then Mum with only her feet in.

"It's freezing," she said.

We all knew she was going to say that. She always says that. To get Mum up to her neck in any kind of water is a big event.

I swam over to Dad. He was standing on the sandy bottom up to his chin in the water. We looked into each other's eyes for a long while. Nobody was doing any backing down.

It was a stand-off.

It looked like it was going to be a long trip.

Coming back we took a closer look at the lady's front yard. She had more than knick-knacks. She had every kind of thingumajig and statue that you could imagine. There were dozens of different kinds of wagon wheels painted in bright colours and standing up with flowers growing around them. There were little wooden trains going nowhere. Small bridges painted red, white and blue. Little doll's houses and huts. Weathervanes, families of wooden ducks heading toward a wooden bullfrog painted pink and brown. Wooden squirrels. Little stage coaches with horses. Canada geese on poles. Beavers. Wooden crows sitting on the eaves of the cabin. An iron deer. Chubby naked babies holding bird baths on their heads. Wooden tulips. Birds with their beaks stuck in the grass. A huge wooden butterfly on a pole with its wings out doing a kind of dive; it was a monarch. A string of little British and Canadian flags between two candy-cane-coloured poles. The flags were making snapping noises in the breeze. And lawn chairs in some of the spaces left between the knick-knacks.

"Did you have a nice cool swim?"

It was the lady's voice. It was the lady asking us if we had had a nice cool swim. But where was she? We all looked around.

Then I saw her.

She was sitting on the lawn, in the midst of the knick-knacks, perfectly still. She was wearing a red, white and blue dress. She was between the stage coaches and two chubby babies with bird baths. At her feet the squirrels and wooden birds were staring at each other.

Afterwards, in the hibachi smoke, Dad made up

this crazy story about how she was actually one of the statues and that she only came alive long enough to rent us the cabin and that not very many people stopped here to rent one of her cabins and that she was so used to sitting there waiting that she turned into one of her own thingumajigs and that he'd bet that when we left the next morning, she'd be sitting there, still as a statue, with the wooden squirrels nibbling at her shoes.

There went Dad with one of those wild stories he'd been telling me all the time. He was treating me like I was about six or something! And he was trying to make it so the woman wasn't even human and that she was just like the knick-knacks on the lawn!

While the rest were getting ready for bed I wandered out front hoping I'd see the lady.

She was sitting on her verandah on a couch with her arms folded looking at *me* looking at the diving monarch. She had pudgy arms and a nice face.

I told her I had done a project in school on the monarch and that this one had the perfect colouring and it was just like a real one.

"My husband Gerald made that. He made all these wood sculptures here. That was his hobby."

"I think they're neat."

"It's hard when your partner leaves you. It's very lonesome. That monarch was one of the last shapes Gerald ever made."

"Did he go away?"

"Oh no, dear. He died you see. And I'm all alone now."

25

I felt so sorry all of a sudden that I couldn't say a thing. My hands went up, or something, and she seemed to know. The next thing I knew she had me in her kitchen offering me cookies and all kinds of home-made goodies. It smelled like a granny's kitchen should smell. A bread-and-clean-tablecloths-and-geranium smell.

I settled for a serviette full of home-made chocolates and went back to our cabin.

I didn't show anybody the chocolates and went to bed.

The lights were out and Mum and Dad were talking about getting up at five. We had driven too many miles in one day they were saying. From now on we'd quit driving by two o'clock and then we could just bum around.

Oh great! Make the trip even longer! Just great!

The transport trucks were thundering by on Highway 17 every few minutes. As each truck went by the lights would shine in our window, and get brighter and brighter until it looked as though a truck was going to drive right over my bed. Then the reflection would sweep over the ceiling and it would be dark again.

Then the crickets.

Then another big truck.

Truck!

Crickets.

Truck!

Crickets.

Dad snoring a little bit. . . .

26

Sleep.

I woke up and heard Dad whistling. When you whistle you're supposed to feel good. I didn't know how he could feel so good in the morning. I wasn't doing any whistling.

I looked out the window. Fog!

We were a few miles down the road and Mum was talking about how disappointed she was about the plastic bags not working. The wind and rain had ripped them and our stuff was all wet. The suitcases were on top of the car with no covering now. All that work for nothing.

"I suppose the lady was on duty with the knick-knacks when we left this morning?" I decided to take a shot at Dad.

"Yeah, she was there alright," Dad said.

'What lady?" Ryan said.

"She *was* there?" I said.

"Yeah," Dad said. "I looked and I didn't see her, so she must have been there, right? Last night when we came back from the swim, we didn't see her either, right? And she *was* there, right? So if you don't see her, she's *there*.Right?"

What an easy put-down of a nice lady, I thought.

"Just a minute, Dad," I said. "I was talking to her last night and her husband Gerald, who made all those neat knick-knacks died and left her all alone and all she has left to remember him by is those knick-knacks, and I think they're beautiful and she makes great home-made chocolates and she's really lonesome and a nice lady."

27

Dad never was very careful of what he said to us those days and I kept believing everything he said and then finding out that what he said wasn't true. I wasn't a kid anymore and I was starting to get quite serious about the difference between truth and lies. I'm not saying that he told lies but I am saying that the truth was sometimes in big trouble when he was fooling around with it.

We stopped at a picnic table on the bank of the Mississauga River. Ryan lit the coals for the hibachi and I went for a little walk along the river to watch the gulls fly without moving their wings. And anyway, I thought I might cry if I had to listen to Dad again. Dad makes me really mad. He can be so mean in a joking way and then laugh and no one's supposed to be hurt. I wished I didn't want to cry so much.

When I got back to the picnic table, a car with its bumper half hanging off drove in to the spot two down from ours. The car was pulling a little trailer. The father got out and slammed his door so hard that the whole car shook and looked like it was going to fall into a hundred pieces of junk. He opened the trailer lid. Then the mother got out. She kicked her door shut harder than the father, and the whole car rattled like it was getting ready to explode. Then one of the back doors opened and a girl about my age got out and a little boy about Ryan's age fell out on top of her. Then the other back door opened and a tall, skinny teenager got out. He had so much hair you couldn't tell what side his face was on. He slammed the door so hard that the lid of the trailer fell closed and the father started to swear. Then somebody started howling inside the car and the mother reached in and yanked out a kid by the arm. The kid was wearing a very heavy diaper around its knees and its nose was full of goobers. They lit a gas stove and started making their breakfast and pitching garbage around and shouting and swearing and crying and arguing and slamming pots and snarling.

I thought I'd do like Dad did and start up a conversation with some strangers. I picked the boy with the head like an eagle's nest. I couldn't help thinking what if I went up to him and said something and it turned out that I was talking to his back instead of his front.

He was leaning on a big litter barrel throwing an empty Coke can up and down in his hand. I picked up a cornflakes box with a picture of a bear on it (there was garbage all over the place) and walked over to the litter barrel. He was leaning on the barrel and standing in the way. He knew I wanted to put the cornflakes box in the barrel but he didn't move. He just threw his Coke can up and down in his hand.

Then with his other hand he opened up his hair and showed me his face. It reminded me of someone pulling back a curtain and looking out of a window.

"Excuse me," I said, and slipped the cornflakes box by him and let it fall into the barrel.

"I'm going to die," he said. He was staring right into my eyes with his eyes.

"I'm going to die next year. The doctor says I have

a year to live. That's why we took this trip. I've got cancer of the blood. The whole family is supposed to do things together. If I wasn't going to die we wouldn't be on this stupid trip. If I wasn't going to die we'd all be at home now and I'd be having a good time."

"I didn't want to come either," I said.

"Are you going to die too?" he asked.

"Not that I know about."

"You probably are and they just didn't tell you. That's the only reason people take these stupid trips. It's because somebody's going to die. They tried it two years ago with my grandmother but she fooled them. She died at the airport and ruined the whole trip."

There were seagulls all over the place because of the garbage. Some of them were flying without moving their wings. They were so close you could almost touch them.

"Ever try to hit a seagull with an empty can?" he said. "You can't! Watch!"

He held his hair open with one hand and fired his Coke can at the closest seagull. He missed.

"See! Want to try?"

He reached into the barrel and brought out an empty bean can with the jagged lid still on it. It was covered with slime and I didn't even want to hold it never mind throw it at a seagull.

But it would be better than talking about dying so I gave it a try. I aimed the best I could at one that was floating the stillest. It was just hanging there with this stupid expression on its face. I fired the bean can.

I nailed another gull, not the one I was aiming at but one that just happened to be flying by and looking the other way. It let out a squawk and a couple of feathers floated down.

"Fantastic!" he shouted through his hair. "Fantastic! Fantastic. Faaaantaaaastic!"

Then he was into the barrel, digging out every can he could find. The cans were coming out like dirt comes out when a dog buries a bone.

"Fantastic!" he shouted into the barrel with a big hollow sound and an echo.

When he had piled up enough ammunition he started firing at the gulls. He was missing every time. Sometimes a gull would follow a sailing can as it fell.

His hair was flying all over the place.

He looked like he was having a good time. He forgot all about me so I strolled back to our picnic table.

I could smell bacon frying.

Everything grew peaceful. The gulls were sailing.

Dad was whistling.

We ate our breakfast, packed and left.

3

Driving along we passed the time with names we saw on the signs. Ryan started reading them off and I jotted them down.

Serpent River, Blind River
Thessalon and Echo Bay.

Ontario has such beautiful names when you fool with them a little bit and make a rhyme.

> *Mum and Dad, Brother Ryan*
> *Drive the car and hear me say;*
> *Serpent River, Blinded River,*
> *Thessalon and Echo Bay!*

We bought pork chops in the A & P in Sault Ste. Marie. A & Ps look the same no matter where you go.

I wished I was home at our own A & P.

When Mum shops in our A & P at home she walks up and down each aisle right through the store before she gets a cart. She spots all the bargains that way. Then she gets a cart and starts throwing stuff in. Cans with dents in them. Big boxes of this and that on sale. Stuff for the freezer. But this time we didn't do that. When Mum wants something in particular she makes a beeline for it. My grandfather told me what a beeline was. When a bee decides he wants to sting you he doesn't fly all over the place. He heads straight for you. Mum made a beeline for the pork chops. We were out of there in about ten seconds. It was a world record A & P trip.

And, on the radio, Roberta was saying:

> *Batchawana Bay,*
> *Watchin' lovers do their thing;*
> *And in Pancake Park,*
> *Listen to Roberta sing!*
> *Wa, Waaaaaa!*

Knife Lake, Marathon full of smoke and chimneys; Little Pic River, looking for a cabin for the night; Jack-Fish Lake, not too expensive, right by the water, off the highway and away from the trucks, a picnic table right beside the door.

"Perfect," Dad said.

"Are we there yet?" I said, and he gave me a look.

There were quite a few cabins along Jack-Fish Lake but it didn't seem too crowded with people. The cabin next to ours was about fifteen steps away.

While we were unloading the car I noticed Ryan standing near the next cabin talking to a window.

"Ryan," Dad shouted. He wanted him to come and help us with the stuff. Ryan came running. He knew that if he didn't help, Dad wouldn't let him light the hibachi and then he'd just die of grief and tragedy!

As he came running towards us, the window he

was talking to came alive. A boy appeared in a red baseball hat. He looked both ways and then soared out the window as if he wanted to fly. With a loud squawk he landed in a crouch, cawed a bit, then ran around the cabin waving his arms like a crow taking off.

Dad was pointing at the huge hydro wires running behind the cabin and curving away up the side of a high rocky hill off in the distance like giant skipping ropes. We could see three towers not counting the one right behind our cabin.

"That line goes for hundreds of miles across country to feed the big centres with electric power."

More education.

He was looking longingly up the power line. You could tell he wanted to walk up there and follow the wires to the third tower. It looked easy from where we were so I offered one of my special kind of apologies (they come a day or two later in a disguised sort of way) for the pickled egg mess.

"Let's walk up the line," I said, trying to sound excited.

Mum gave me that look that says, "My aren't you a thoughtful girl."

I gave her right back my special look where I curl up my lip that says, "OK, but don't make a big thing of it!"

We had to wait until Ryan got on long pants and lit the hibachi. Then we took off.

We walked straight back over the train tracks and across a field until we were standing right under the wires. Then we started following them.

Through some tall bushes and down into a gulley we walked in single file. Suddenly we came on a creek.

And a red baseball hat.

He had his back to us. Under the hat he had black hair jutting out. The kind of hair I like, thick and wavy. He was a little shorter than me but I could tell by the way he stood he was a lot stronger. He had on checkered pants, North Stars and a Kung Fu shirt on backwards. He was standing beside the creek with his legs apart and his hands together holding something in front of him.

Then he turned around.

In both hands he had dripping gobs of fungus from the edge of the creek. He went down in another crouch, his hands full of fungus almost touching the ground.

"THERE'S FUNGUS AMONG US!" he shouted, and threw his handfuls of fungus up in the air. It fell like rain in bits and chunks all around him.

"There's fung-gus amung-gus!"

I just stood there.

He had big brown eyes and he stared right at me. He looked like he was going to laugh.

Then he ran up the creek a bit, turned into the bushes and was gone!

The trip up the line was a bit harder than it looked. What looked like grass from a distance turned out to be brambles and bushes up to my chin with big broken rocks and holes. Some places were so steep we had to crawl on our hands and knees to get any-where. The flies were having a picnic. Black flies mostly. One time Mum read us a thing in a magazine where a man was killed by black flies in northern Ontario. I could believe it.

At the second tower we sat down on some bare rock and leaned on the steel of the tower and looked for the first time back down the line.

We could see the cabin, Jack-Fish Lake, the car, another mountain and the train track disappearing around it.

And I could see the red baseball hat near our cabin.

"Fungus among us? Is that what he said?"

"That's what it sounded like," Dad said.

"Look at the neat insulators!" Ryan said.

The third tower was impossible so we headed back.

Not too long after we could smell the A & P pork chops sizzling we jumped into Jack-Fish Lake.

Mum came down too and stuck her foot in.

Later that evening I was lying on top of my bed making notes and reading a comic when someone knocked on the door.

I never should have answered it.

It was Ryan. He's done this dozens of times. And I always fall for it. I guess it's because I'm always expecting someone exciting.

He knocks at the door and when you open it he says politely "thank you", then laughs like a maniac and walks right in, stomping on your foot as hard as he can on his way. Really hilarious!

There he was. But it was different this time. He

didn't come right in. He stood there with a funny look on his face.

"Do you like that guy with the red baseball cap?"

"What?"

"Do you like that guy with the red baseball cap?"

"What do you want to know for?"

"It's a dare."

"What if I say I don't?"

"Then I win."

"OK. I do."

"You gotta say it all."

"OK. I like the guy with the red baseball cap."

Then Ryan looked behind the open cabin door and said, "OK, you can come out now!"

I heard some scurrying and a red hat flashed around the corner.

Ryan makes me feel mad and silly and small when he tricks me like that. I hate dumb boys!

I chased Ryan for almost an hour with a big stick. Then we all went to bed.

Much later, I was lying there dreaming I was awake. I started out dreaming I was asleep. Then I started to dream I was awake. I could hear the water in Jack-Fish Lake making slurping noises against the shore. It was dark in our cabin but bright outside because of the moon.

Suddenly, outside the screen door, a shape appeared. There was somebody standing out there looking in the screen door!

It was a screen door with one of those long springs

on the inside to make it slam. I used to twang the one at my uncle's cottage and pretend it was a guitar.

Then I heard the spring stretch. The door was being opened!

Just the slightest stretching sound of the spring and everything else quiet as moonlight.

I started wiggling my toes like mad to see if I was awake.

The form slipped in the door and eased it closed with just a slight creak of the spring.

When he turned in the doorway trying to get his eyes used to the dark, I could see the shape of a baseball hat.

It was the red hat!

I let my eyelashes come down so my eyes looked closed. I was looking through my lashes and I could see everything. It was like spying on somebody through tall grass.

My heart was jumping all over the place.

He moved like a ghost over to where Mum and Dad were sleeping. Then he floated over to Ryan's bed.

I was next!

I held my breath and kept watching through my lashes. I was going to hold my breath until I couldn't hold it any longer ... then I was going to scream blue murder!

He was right beside my bed now.

I could see the outline of the cap.

Then he bent over me and blocked out the light from the moon in the doorway.

I felt something soft touching my lips. He was kissing me right on the lips!

Then he tore out the door and the old spring really did the job! The slam sounded like a gun going off.

Everybody sat up in bed at once.

"What the hell is that!" Dad said.

'It was the wind blowing the screen door," I said.

Everybody fell back on their beds.

Dad went back to sleep muttering something about how wind can't blow a screen door.

Mum made a sort of purring noise as she snuggled back up to Dad.

Soon everybody was back to sleep again.

Except me.

4

We had juice and toast and jam in our cabin early and cleaned up and left.

When you're anywhere with Mum you usually leave a place cleaner than you found it. But Mum doesn't do it all. Nobody is anybody's servant around our house when there's cleaning up to do. People clean up their own messes. I notice at most of my friends' places the mother is the champion cleaner and the kids and the father just leave everything lying around. Not our place. When there's cleaning up around our place it's like being on the program "Emergency". Everybody's running around like there's a bomb scare or something. We were all pretty good at it except Ryan. Not that he wasn't trying hard. It's just that it's hard to do all that stuff with your eyes closed. Dad was teasing Mum a bit about it. He was looking under the bed for specks of dust but she didn't pay any attention to him. Then he picked a little feather that was sticking out of one of the pillows and said, "What about this?" but she ignored him.

There was a sign over the sink that read, "Clean your own dishes or leave 50¢."

We didn't need to leave a cent.

As we left I looked for a beautiful boy in a red hat. I'd like to be able to say I saw him but I can't.

We always left places so early that we never saw a soul.

It bothered me that I would never see him again. Not ever. Not the rest of my life. I'd never see my grandfather again either. Never. All I was allowed to do was to remember. And that was hard. I could hardly remember Grandpa's face. But a song, or a taste of some kinds of stew or the smell of something like a certain kind of pipe tobacco would make him and his face come back for a minute. But that's all they'd let you have. It bothered me. That's all you'd ever get of some things.

Red hats. Red baseball hats. When I see a red baseball hat I still think of him and I can see him. Nothing else will do it. Except fungus sometimes.

We were fooling around with the radio and watching Lake Superior. Highway 17 was doing its best to fall over one of the cliffs into the rough water. The wind was raising the spray away up in the air when the water hit the rocks and the waves had white foam on them away out across the water. It looked like an ocean, not a lake.

The big trucks were multiplying. They seemed to travel in pairs. One would pass and blow you all over the road and just when he'd get by you another one would roar up beside you and spill out black smoke all over the car.

Dad was hanging on to the steering wheel very tight. I could tell by how white his hands were. Mum was fiddling with the radio listening to people talk.

I was glad Dad was suffering for a change and not whistling. It was about time. If I was going to suffer, why shouldn't he?

We heard about a celebration somewhere around Terrace Bay that had something to do with a big American company that was going to cut down all the trees in Ontario but that was not going to pollute anything while they were doing it.

We also heard of a big convention of Satan's Choice motorcycle riders that was being held in Thunder Bay. We listened to a phone-in show where everybody was saying they should go somewhere else for their convention.

More trucks ganged up on us and Dad was getting crabby. We were looking for a picnic table to have a brunch but along that stretch of Highway 17 they don't seem to care about people who want to stop and relax.

It wasn't until the wind from a huge truck full of steel things blew a suitcase off our car that Dad decided to pull off on a side road and have a rest.

Ryan noticed the suitcase first. We heard a scraping rumbling noise and Ryan looked out the back window and yelled.

I turned and saw the suitcase turning over and over in the air almost like in slow motion! It turned about five times in the air, then hit the highway and bounced straight back up in the air and started to tumble again. Then it hit the road again and bounced, but not so high this time. The next time it bounced a lot lower and then settled on the road and spun around like a top. Before it stopped spinning a huge transport appeared and hit it on the edge with its front wheel and gave it another ride in the air.

We pulled off the road and Dad walked back and picked it up. We watched him go. His head was down and his shoulders were stooped over. He was feeling rotten. He got back finally and the trucks were roaring by, shaking the car each time with the wind they made.

We drove slowly down the road, letting the cars and trucks pile up behind us in a big line. We finally turned off on a dirt road near a gravel pit and stopped.

"Great trip, eh Mum?" I said loud enough so everybody in the whole district could hear.

Dad didn't say a word.

He got out, opened the back, went into the cooler, got out two beers and sat in the weeds and gravel and grass and opened one. Then he opened another one. Ryan and I threw stones for a while. There was a roaring sound of motorcycles down the gravel road. And dust rising.

In about an hour we were in Thunder Bay at a picnic table in a small park near the water.

We were making a cheese omelette in a pan on the hibachi and fooling around watching freight trains go slowly by when a police car pulled up behind our car and shut off his motor.

He was talking on his radio and Ryan's mouth fell open. He was over there in a second.

"Everything alright, folks?" the policeman said.

Dad slipped his can of beer behind some Coke cans on the table.

"Fine," he said.

"See any gangs in leather rodding around?"

"No."

"We had some trouble here last night with hoods on motorcycles."

"Satan's Choice?"

"Right. Do you know anything about Satan's Choice?"

"Oh sure. We drove all the way from Ottawa to attend their convention," Dad said and gave his little laugh but the policeman didn't seem to understand it. Dad and his humour, I thought.

The policeman got on his radio and told somebody where he was.

Dad got a lot more friendly. He walked over to the car and introduced himself.

"I'm Constable O'Neil," the policeman answered but he didn't stick his hand out of the car to shake Dad's.

"Can you show my little boy here some of the equipment you use? He'd love to see it and we'll be leaving soon. Travelling all the way across Canada. Having a great time."

"Can you show my *little boy*." What about his little girl? The two great chums. Terrific.

Constable O'Neil smiled and brightened up a bit. My Dad. What a charmer. Terrific.

Ryan was in the car in one second. He got to turn

on the two cherries on top and make them flash. He worked a handle from the inside and made a big spotlight turn around to search for crooks in the bushes at night. He turned on the two special fog lights on the fenders. And another big spotlight attached on the door. And a hand light which Constable O'Neil saved until last. (I think he was more impressed with his lights than even Ryan was.) And then finally, his most famous light! It was like a taxi sign on top and said STOP POLICE! when you pushed a switch.

Ryan was in heaven. So was Constable O'Neil.

So was Dad.

I wasn't.

Constable O'Neil also showed him his gun and ammunition belt and his stick for smashing you on the head, his siren which he rang once and his bullhorn which Ryan got to speak through. Ryan said, "This is Ryan! Hear this, this is Ryan!"

Constable O'Neil finally had to take it away from him. They were all acting like a bunch of kids when the car radio came on and the Constable said he had to go.

"Don't go near that Satan's Choice gang, sir, they are very bad people. A family was beaten up last night in this park."

Then he drove away, spinning his wheels and raising a huge sheet of dust.

Dad got his beer out from behind the Coke cans and finished it.

I probably didn't say anything but it was in the air.

In the air was "Let's hope we get wherever we're going without getting beaten up!"

By noon we were in Thunder Bay watching the grain trains and the long oil ships and listening to the whistling and honking and watching the smoke.

The radio was talking about forest fires burning all over Ontario, especially in Quetico Provincial Park near where we were.

I was getting more sad and scared. Fires, police, people getting beaten up, trucks knocking us around, dust, noise, huge machines, heat, the wind howling in Dad's half open window . . .

I slept and so did Ryan, all the way to Upsala. When I woke up, Mum was driving. When Mum drives she talks a lot. She says she talks to keep herself from being nervous. She was telling us about jobs she had before she got married. Her uncle was a fridge salesman and she had a job standing beside a fridge at some fridge show opening the door every time somebody wanted to look inside at the shelves and the light going on and stuff. Then she had a job counting paperback books in a big warehouse someplace and she used to read the books on her lunch hour and that was where she started to get a big vocabulary.

The trucks were getting worse. The worse the trucks got the more she talked about jobs. She worked at a summer lodge where all the rich people went and the golf teacher there was showing her how to swing a golf club and she hit the pastry chef on the head with it by mistake.

Dad said if we could get to Wabigoon the worst part of the whole trip would be over. Wabigoon. It looked so far on our map. I listened to the radio man talking about more fires and watched Mum getting attacked by transport trucks. One behind us, one in front of us, one passing us.

What scenery! Travel across Canada! See the countryside!

Sure Dad, sure!

I woke up outside the A & P in Dryden. For a minute I thought we were back in Ottawa. We made a beeline for fresh corn on the cob, fat weiners, home-made bread and went looking for a cabin.

It was supper time. Ryan and I started to fight. We were covered with sweat. The road was under con-struction and there was nothing but dust. Dad was driving again. I had a headache and felt sick. The in-side of the car was sticky and filthy.

I checked the map again. Would we ever get out of Ontario? I hated Ontario. This was our third day in this stupid province. Dad said he thought Ontario was bigger than all of Europe. I hated Europe too. I hated roads and Ryan and trucks and noise and pine trees and Ryan and Ontario.

We drove further over some hills and the air started getting cooler and the road started winding and it got a lot quieter.

Then we got to Big Eagle Lake.

We drove right up beside a cabin near the water and got out. Dad lay down on his back on the cool grass with his arms and legs spread apart. Mum lay down on the grass too. Then I lay down. Then Ryan.

Nobody said anything for a long time. The clouds were walking along slowly like lazy sheep. A squirrel was telling us all about the place.

"HOLY SHIT, is this ever beautiful!" Dad said.

"Is it all right if I say 'shit'?" I said.

"Just this once," Dad said.

"Oh shit!" I said. "Is this ever beautiful."

"Shit, is it ever," Mum said.

"What about me?" Ryan said.

"What *about* you?" Dad said.

"Oh shit, oh shit, oh shit, oh shit ... " Ryan said.

Ryan always overdoes everything.

We wrapped the corn in butter and foil. The home-made bread we wrapped in butter, garlic and foil. The fat weiners we didn't have to wrap. They were in their own skins already and sizzling.

We swam.

Even Mum went in up to her chest and let the water pour down the front of her bathing suit. Then she ran out.

We were finishing the fat weiners and the corn when the man who ran the place asked us if we wanted to go fishing with him. It was all part of something called the "American Plan" we were on. It included cabin, breakfast, bait and the use of a boat and a small motor.

I asked Dad why it was called the American Plan. He said he didn't know and he didn't care.

"Not very educational," I said, smiled and walked away.

I can be very sarcastic when I want to be.

Ryan and Dad were out in the boat with the man and Mum and I were talking and swatting mosquitoes. Then the moon started and so did the crickets.

The pine trees were sticking up into the moonlight.

Mum said she'd stay there the rest of her life if she had to.

I asked her if she found the water cold when it ran down the front of her bathing suit so fast. She said that she did and out of the corner of my eye I saw a nice look on her face in the moonlight.

"I notice you're starting to get a little room down the front of *your* bathing suit too."

I was trying to think of something adult to say when my favorite bird said it for me.

"Whip-poor-will."

The thing I like about whip-poor-wills is that they save you from speaking sometimes when you're stuck for something to say.

We could hear the putt-putt of the motor. The fishermen were coming back.

We ran down to the dock to meet them. Ryan was yelling and screaming like a maniac about a fish.

The man who ran the place threw a fish on the dock that was taller than Ryan if it could have stood up. There was blood running down its side.

"Average muskie you catch around here," the man said. "We use minnows. Wanna see 'em?"

We all looked in the minnow pail that he was taking out of the boat and tying to the side of the dock. There were about twenty-five minnows in there, poking their noses into the side of the pail.

After everybody raved about the fish for about half an hour we went up to the cabin and got ready for bed.

"Whip-poor-will ... whip-poor-will ... whip-poor-will ... "

So so silent. Just the crickets and my favorite bird.

We turned out the lights and everybody was snoozing in about one minute except me.

I got up and squeezed into my wet bathing suit. I sneaked out and walked down on the cold grass to the dock. It was slippery with scales and fish slime and some blood. I sat down with my feet in the deep water and a bit of a chill up my back.

I opened the minnow pail and raised it a bit so that the water tilted and I could see the minnows flipping against the side. I cupped one in my hand and eased him into the lake. He dove headfirst into the black water with a little slurp. A little silver flash of moonlight and a slurp.

I let every one of them go.

Then I let myself down into the lake and hung onto the dock with my hands and let the water come up to my chin.

Some of it went down the front of my bathing suit. But not much.

I went back to the cabin, got into my pyjamas and snuggled into bed.

The whip-poor-will is beautiful music to go to sleep to.

I loved Ontario that night.

5

I was the last one asleep and the first one awake. When you do that you feel like you've been alone for a long, long time. You feel as though nobody knows the things *you* know. You feel special and kind of excited.

Besides, I was making plans to run away.

Ryan was completely under the covers in his bed. He always sleeps like that. He starts off like a normal person with the covers up to his chin and his arms outside the blankets. By the time morning comes he is completely covered, except for his feet. His feet are on the pillow and his head is down at the other end. It's a wonder he doesn't smother. When he wakes up he gets in a panic and usually claws his way out the bottom where the sheets are tucked in. When his head finally comes out he blinks his eyes about a hundred times and looks around like our cats do when you turn on the light in a dark room where they've been sleeping. After he figures himself out, he flops back up where he started the night before and has another snooze.

Dad and Mum usually do a chair when they sleep. Dad lies on his side with his knees up so that he's shaped like a chair. Mum lies on her side and sits in the chair. Dad's arms are around her. He won't do it if she wears curlers though, because the back of her head is stuck right in his face. When she's got the curlers on she has to be the chair.

The man who owned the place rang a gong and we went over to the main lodge for breakfast. We were the only guests. He told us that he usually had a big crowd there from Chicago but that something was wrong in America and they didn't come this year.

A lady served us a huge breakfast and I asked Dad if that was the man's wife. He said it was.

"How do you know?"

"Because she looks like him."

"You mean when people are married they look alike?"

"Not right away, but if they hang around with each other long enough they start imitating each other and they end up looking the same."

I knew I was walking into something but I walked into it anyway.

"How come you and Mum don't look alike?"

"We do. See?" Then he put on his stupid face where he sticks his chin out as far as it will go and he has this stupid grin on him.

I looked at Mom. She was doing the same thing.

They looked alike, alright. Like a couple of dopes. Especially Dad.

Fortunately, nobody else was in the place or I would have been really embarrassed.

We were back on Highway 17 and getting some Manitoba radio stations. Manitoba seemed like another country to me before I got there. We started travelling on Monday morning and here it was Thursday morning and we were still in Ontario. I wondered if everything would change when we crossed the border.

Dad said he didn't think it would. He said we wouldn't notice.

We passed a statue of an Indian. This one was huge. Dad stopped the car and we went over and stood beside the Indian. My head didn't reach his knee. He had on a skin tied around his waist. It was made of wood just carved to look like a skin. Around the back was a bare bum. I didn't look under the front. Ryan said there was nothing there anyway.

His face was ugly. Big fangs hung down where his teeth should have been. One arm pointed straight out and the hand was turned so that the fingers made a fist but the thumb was pointing straight up.

I wonder why people who make statues of Indians have to make them look like that!

Imagine! A huge statue of an Indian making an insult with his thumb right on the side of Highway 17 where almost everybody passes sometime or other. That whole statue is an insult. I wonder how Indians feel when they drive down Highway 17.

On the radio we were listening to news about some real Indians. They had captured a park in the middle of the town of Kenora and we were heading right for them.

Mum's map of Ontario was getting pretty worn out. She had it folded about a million different ways and it was full of pencil marks and holes along the folds.

"I'll certainly be glad to divest myself of this Ontario map and start on the Manitoba one," she said.

We stopped in Kenora a couple of times and asked some people where the park was that the Indians had captured. They all said they weren't from Kenora, they were from somewhere else.

Then we saw the park. We knew it was the park because we saw a television camera truck parked beside it. That's all we saw. The television truck.

And the radio kept saying there was a war going on in Kenora. All we saw was tourists.

Some war!

The fires were still burning in Quetico.

There was a Ukrainian Festival in Dauphin, Manitoba, the radio said.

There was a frog jumping contest in Winnipeg.

We had already attended the Satan's Choice convention in Thunder Bay.

What a social life you can have on the radio!

By the time we got to the Manitoba border everybody had to pee. Except Mum. Mum never has to pee. Or, I should say, she can hold in the longest. You can tell when she has to go badly. She doesn't want you to talk to her. She doesn't jiggle around or start looking for a place or anything. She just says, "Nobody talk to me, because I won't answer you." Then, of course, Dad starts talking to her about all sorts of things.

When Dad has to go, it's all of a sudden. All of a

sudden he pulls the car over, anywhere, and gets out. If there's no bush or anything to hide behind, he goes anyway. Right beside the car.

Boys are lucky.

When we got back in the car, Dad started talking.

"Notice how the whole thing changes so suddenly as soon as you get across the border? Soon as you cross it the road gets wider and the land gets flatter. And look, they have round junk cans on the side of the road. They call them 'orbits'. You throw your junk in them so that you don't litter. And the bush on the side of the road is gone. And so are the hills. The land is getting flatter by the minute."

"Dad," I said, "you said it would change gradually and it's not. It's changing all of a sudden!"

"I did not!"

"You did so!"

"Ask Mum!"

"Don't talk to me, because I won't answer you!"

We drove on some more, all of us in silence.

The land got flatter and flatter. The earth got blacker and blacker.

A train off in the distance looked like a toy. When you see a train in Manitoba you see the whole train. Ryan counted the cars. More than one hundred. And it looked like a toy, two engines, caboose and all.

And we were through with Highway 17. We were on Highway 1 now.

The road was so straight that Dad was only touching the steering wheel with one finger. It seemed like we were sailing on water. And we were so tiny. Almost like looking at the map and feeling like a little bug or a germ or something smaller even. Here we were in a dinky little model of a car. Four tiny midgets driving along on a toy highway in a dinky car.

The big toy was all there, all except the giant who ran the whole thing ... who made it go.

I was starting to worry again.

Dad was telling us about Portage and Main. He said that was the main corner in Winnipeg. If you stand on the corner of Portage Avenue and Main Street long enough, you'll meet somebody you know because it's supposed to be the crossroads of Canada. Sure, Dad. Everybody in Canada goes there sometime in their lives.

"Everybody, Dad?"

"Everybody. Specially your friends and acquaintances. If you stand there long enough, somebody you recognize will come along."

We could see Winnipeg. We'd be there in a minute.

About an hour later we could *still* see Winnipeg. We'd be there in no time.

We stopped and threw some junk into "orbit".

"We'll be in Winnipeg in no time, Mum."

No answer.

More toy houses, trains, trucks, cars, airplanes.

And tiny people off in the distance. And toothpick telephone poles with little threads for wires. And the sky as big as the ocean. You lie on your back and look at the ocean out the window. One little cloud away up stays with you. You are flying over the ocean, looking down on the blue water. Your airplane is humming a little bit and the blue air is whispering at the window.

I slept until the car stopped at a parking lot around the corner from Portage and Main in Winnipeg. Ryan and Mum headed for a snack bar in the bottom of a big hotel. Mum was practically running. Ryan was trotting behind her. It was obvious where they were going.

"We'll meet you there," she shouted over the noise of the cars.

Dad and I stood under the sign that said Portage and Main and started to wait.

It was lunch time and thousands of people were passing by, four different ways, at Portage and Main. Thousands of people and hundreds of cars. The streets were the widest I'd ever seen.

I searched each face for someone I knew.

One old man looked like my grandfather who died and my heart sank. It wasn't him. Then a RED BASEBALL HAT came bobbing through the crowd and my heart stopped. No. It was just some girl in a red hat.

Dad was looking each way as the lights changed. And the people flowed past like a river.

He smoked two cigarettes.

The time was passing.

By this time I knew everybody. I knew people I hadn't ever met. I knew people that I just made up.

I was looking up Portage and Dad was looking down Main.

"As I live and breathe," I heard him shout, "fancy meeting you here, of all places!"

It couldn't be. Had it really happened?

I turned around so fast I almost fell over.

It was Ryan and Mum.

Dad went on. There was no stopping him.

"What on earth are you doing in this neck of the woods? Isn't this the most *incredible* coincidence! What a small world this really is! How in the world *are* you anyway? I haven't seen you in a *dog's* age! And is *this* little Ryan? I can't believe how he's grown!" He pinched Ryan's cheek.

People were starting to stare at us.

Ryan and Mum were looking at each other wondering what was up.

Dad wouldn't quit, and people were really looking now.

"You must remember my daughter? I guess the last time you saw *her* she was knee high to a *grass-hopper*. Here we were just standing here on the corner of Portage and Main, having a rest on our way to the Pacific Ocean, and right out of the blue we run into ..."

I was so embarrassed I wanted to disappear.

Mum grabbed him by the shirt.

"To the car," she said, "before they come along with a net and take you away!"

They were still laughing when we got out of the other side of Winnipeg and into the country again.

But I wasn't. I was in a panic. I felt like my stomach had jumped into my mouth.

"You know, Dad, I really *did* see someone I knew at Portage and Main," I said.

"You did not."

"Yes I did. In fact I saw hundreds of people I knew if you want to know."

"You saw hundreds of people you knew at Portage and Main?" I was starting to cry.

"Yes. Hundreds and hundreds."

"What's *she* crying about now?" Dad said.

6

In Portage la Prairie we bought fresh vegetables, beautiful corn and carrots and green onions, cold beer, and about four thousand raspberries.

Then we started north on the Yellowhead Road.

The radio was selling things. Not like they do in Ontario with ads and songs and stupid verses and stuff. This was more like want ads.

For sale. Two persian pussies. Mother and daughter. Apply so and so, Gladstone, Manitoba.

While they sold things on the radio, I filled my face with raspberries.

In Gladstone we started looking. In our hotel book five stars meant a hotel was just wonderful. We found a hotel in Gladstone with *no* stars.

We didn't want a hotel or motel anyway. We wanted cabins. Cabins beside water.

We were still talking about travelling and meeting people and coincidences and "fate" as Mum put it. She said that she met Dad through "fate". She forgot her purse at somebody's place and went back about an hour later and went in the living room and looked up and there HE was standing beside a tall lamp and the light was shining on the side of his face. If she hadn't forgotten her purse that time she would never have met Dad. And we wouldn't be here.

None of this would be happening! All because of a purse!

I wondered who I would have been if she hadn't taken a purse to that party, or if there had only been short lamps, and she could only have seen Dad's feet. I wondered if it wasn't for that old purse, if she would have married someone whose idea of a holiday was just to stay in his back yard and read while his daughter played with her friends.

I decided to bug Ryan, who was sitting quietly in a trance, listening to this great love story.

With a mouthful of raspberries I said, "What if we stopped at this bakery here in Gladstone, Manitoba, and Ryan met a little girl and spoke to her, and then fifteen years later he married somebody away back in Ottawa and it turned out to be her? Just think, Ryan, you might meet the love of your life, right here, in this bake shop in Gladstone, Manitoba!"

"Why don't you shut up?" Ryan said.

Dad and I hadn't had any lunch and the bakery smelled delicious and we bought some beautiful bread and raisin buns and Dad tore a big chunk out of one of the buns right there in front of the lady and gave me some and we ate it right there and told the lady what a fantastic cook she was and she blushed and laughed and the little girl about Ryan's age that he might marry by fate someday was nowhere in sight. And then we drove off hunting for a cabin by some water.

There are no cabins by the water in that part of Manitoba.

I ate more raspberries.

We were fed up looking when we finally stopped at a fancy looking motel in Minnedosa. The sign said:

COLOUR TV

HEATED POOL AND SAUNA

AIR CONDITIONING

CLOSED CIRCUIT BABY SITTER.

"We have to stay here," Dad said. "I'm not driving another inch."

In the room Mum was fiddling with the TV. One channel had on a picture of a pool.

"That's the baby sitter!" I said. "The kids go in the pool and the adults stay here in the room and watch the kids swim on TV."

"How electronically unifying for all of us," Mum said.

In one second, Ryan and I were outside, across the grass and into the building where the indoor pool was. Mum had told us to wave or something when we got there. Ryan and I got in the empty pool and waved like mad towards the little camera, then dashed back to the room to see if they had seen us. They hadn't. They had on another channel and were watching President Nixon sweat.

I switched channels for them and we ran back and I did a funny dive for the camera while Ryan made faces and pretended he was drowning.

We ran back to see what they'd say.

They were watching President Nixon waving from an airplane.

I switched it again and ran back.

This time I'd get their attention.

I did two of my specialty dives. That's the one where I swim along and when I'm right close to the camera I duck under the water and let my behind stick up while I pull down the bottom of my two-piece bathing suit at the same time.

I ran back.

I met Dad on the way.

"Guess what?" he said, "They say Nixon is going to resign."

"Weren't you watching the pool? I did a specialty dive for you!"

"No. I was watching Walter Cronkite."

"What kind of a father are you anyway? My first TV appearance and you're watching Walter Cronkite on another channel!"

We all went back to the pool, except Mum, and dove in. After we swam around for a while Dad said, "Anyway, I've seen your bare bum before. It's nothing new for me. But I guess the people in the other hotel rooms might have found it interesting."

My face got as red as the Manitoba sunset was going to be that night.

Dad and Ryan cackled and laughed and fell down and choked for about an hour.

The people who owned that motel loved signs. There were signs in the bathroom about what not to throw down the toilet and what to do with the shower curtain. There were signs telling you how to turn on the lights and how to use the radio and the TV and the phone and they were all "Do Not" signs. It reminded me of school. A sign outside the room said "DO NOT BAR-B-Q". Inside the room a sign said "DO NOT EAT INSIDE MOTEL ROOM".

Mum turned the sign around and we sat down on the wall-to-wall rug, in the air conditioning, and ate a feast of home-made bread, green onions, cold meat, mayonnaise, pickled eggs, lettuce, dills, radishes, plums, beer, Coke, donuts and smarties. And raspberries.

Then we sat up in bed and watched a movie on TV with Humphrey Bogart pulling bloodsuckers off his legs on an old steamboat in Africa. Yuccch!

Then we went to bed.

If Dad has more than four beers before he goes to bed he snores.

He snored that night.

But I woke up yelling louder than any snoring. First, I woke up puking, then I started yelling.

I was yelling for Mum but I only got the name out once. The next thing I did was throw up again, red, all over the sheets.

This is blood, I thought, and I'm going to die. I'm only a young woman and there's so much I want to do and I'm too young to die.

After the basins and the rags and the mess I got back into Dad's and Mum's bed.

Here I was on a trip I didn't even want to come on in the first place!

And I was dying! Maybe that guy was right.

Maybe that's why Dad said we had to go on this trip.

I could be DYING!

Dad opened the drawer in the table beside the bed and pulled out a book.

"See if it says anything in here about raspberries," he said, and gave me a little pat.

It was a Gideon Bible.

He can be sarcastic when he wants to be.

Ryan brought me a cold cloth for my head.

He's kind, Ryan, when he's serious, and even he must have known that this was serious.

We left the hotel as usual, cleaner than we found it. Except for my sheets.

We took off again, heading for the Pacific.

While they had breakfast at a picnic ground on the way to the Saskatchewan border, I lay beside the picnic table under a blanket with ice cubes from the cooler wrapped in a cloth on my head.

I saw Dad and Ryan go for a walk while Mum fried some eggs. I watched them walk across the prairie and I could tell they were talking.

Wasn't that just great! Here I was sick as a dog and Dad all of a sudden picks this time to go running off across the prairie with his favorite "little man" to have a real "boys" talk and do "boys" things. They'd probably go chasing gophers or have a stupid race or see who could throw a stone the farthest or who could climb a tree (there weren't any trees there but who cares) and shoot pretend guns at each other and hide from those stupid late movie Indians and dig holes and look for treasure and get filthy. Great!

I hoped they'd get lost or bitten to death by an

insane army of rabid rattlesnakes.

I stuck my head under my blanket and Mum ate breakfast all by herself.

It was still early morning when we left for the border. The road was cutting through fields of mustard and rapeseed. The yellow colour of the mustard and the rapeseed was so yellow it didn't seem real. We have some pictures of paintings by Peter Breughel on our walls at home. In some of them he has some unbelievable yellow fields. The fields in Manitoba of rapeseed and mustard looked like that.

Maybe it was because I was sick, but they didn't seem like real fields.

Rapeseed and mustard are ugly names for fields so beautiful.

I slept and woke.

I slept and woke the way you do when you're off school sick at home and you feel like you're floating and you think you're somewhere else and maybe you hear people's voices outside, or a cat crying, or somebody whistling or an airplane buzzing and you find a cool place for your cheek on the pillow and you wiggle your toes and go to sleep again just for a minute.

It's nice being sick sometimes.

I woke up and the car was stopped on the prairie in the middle of two fields, one blue, one yellow. A sign on the roadside marked the Saskatchewan border.

I was lying on my back looking at the map. Between Ottawa and Vancouver I drew a line with my eye. We were right in the middle of the line.

There was hardly any traffic and Dad and Ryan were talking about the big farm machinery we were passing on our way. Then Dad pulled over beside a huge combine and everybody but me got out to see if the farmer would show it to them. They were out there for about half an hour. When they got back in I started to mumble as though I had one of those jungle fevers you see in old TV movies.

With little moans and groans as I talked, I said: "Where am I? Somebody tell me where I am! I looked out the window and I saw a red machine big as a house parked beside us. On top of it there were two men. They were in a little glass room. One had a red face and he looked like a Martian. And the other one looked like Dad. And then a little monkey crawled up there and it looked like Ryan!"

They just ignored me.

We drove on to the town of Yorkton and I did it again.

"Where am I? I looked out the window and I saw a huge farmer with thumbs as big as red balloons!"

No effect.

They ignored me.

If we were only on this trip because I was going to die, they sure weren't making my last days much fun — or even acting like they cared.

We bought a bunch of postcards and started driving again. Mum was looking over the Saskatchewan map for a picnic table. She found one, and I began to feel almost better.

Ryan was being nice to me. I didn't say thanks to

him or try to kiss him or anything because I knew
he didn't like that kind of thing.

Near the town of Wadena at the Lion's Club picnic
area, Ryan wrote his first French postcard to his
friend Mike in Ottawa.

Cher Michel

Je suis à Lions Club table pic-a-nic.
J'ai vu un petit train.

RYAN

Mum made bar-b-q bacon sandwiches with lettuce
and mayonnaise and pickles and Dad and Ryan carried me into some shady bushes and put me down on
a blanket. I had cool lemonade and listened to the
heat bugs screaming. They were talking about how
sick I was.

"SEEEEEEEEEEEK! SEEEEEEEEEK! SHE'S
SEEEEEEEK!"

I heard Dad and Ryan talking quietly. I knew they
were concerned about me.

I was feeling better and better and I was hungry
but I left part of my sandwich anyway, for effect.

The better I got the more I realized that the only
part of the trip I had enjoyed was when I was sick.

Being sick is being a queen.

The sign that said Lion's Club Picnic Area was
broken and falling down. The top of the picnic table
was rotting and the grass was growing up through the
holes.

An old-fashioned water pump half covered in tall

grass and without a handle looked pretty sad.

The heat bugs were still singing at me when we left and I was busy feeling sorry for the poor old lions in the Lion's Club.

We were travelling through the middle of Saskatchewan north of Tête Jaune and counting the miles between elevators. From a distance, grain elevators look like milk cartons. Ryan was counting the miles between milk cartons. He figured eleven miles between each one by watching the speedometer. I agreed with him. But I measured differently. I measured by the songs on the radio. During the hit parade, four songs, plus all the talking, would be about eleven miles.

The radio had a song on about death.

> *Billy don't be a hero*
> *Don't be a fool with your life . . .*

It must be awful to die. What if the raspberry juice had been blood!

What if I were really dying!

What if I die here.

Then I'd be taken to the nearest hospital, probably in Yorkton, Saskatchewan, and Mum and Ryan and Dad would wait in the waiting room for a long time and the doctor would finally come out and say very softly, "She's gone," and Ryan would start to cry and Mum would hug him and cry too and Dad would go over to the window to be brave.

Then my funeral, back home in Ottawa, with me

in the coffin and all my friends lined up to see me and I'd look so pretty but kind of white, and they'd all cry and wonder why it had to happen to me because I was so young and smart and beautiful, and my aunts and uncles would shake their heads and my grandmother would start moaning and praying and then Ryan would ruin it all and mention how the trip was spoiled because of my death and I'd get up out of the coffin and slam him over the head with a big pot of fake flowers and everybody'd start screaming . . .

I was laughing a little bit out loud and tears were running down my face.

"Dad," Ryan whispered, "I think she's gone crazy."

> *Billy, don't be a hero*
> *Don't be a fool with your life,*
> *Billy don't be a hero,*
> *Come back and make me your wife.*

Funny, how dying and loving somebody are often mentioned together.

In Saskatoon, every motel and hotel was full. We were attending another convention. This time it was the Jehovah Witnesses.

When Jehovah Witnesses come to our door at home, Mum always buys their little paper and she's always really nice to them but she won't let them in.

"What a time for a pray-in," Mum said.

In the lobby of a small motel we were talking to a lady and her husband.

"There are no rooms in Saskatoon anywhere, my dear. The city's full of holy rollers!"

Her husband just sat there staring at the TV.

"Isn't it full of holy rollers, Arthur?"

Arthur kept watching the TV. Then Dad started.

"We are all the way from Ottawa and our daughter here is very sick and we can't go another inch."

I tried looking as sick as I could. I let my mouth droop down and my eyes look hazy and I let my breath out so I'd look as pale as I could.

Arthur was watching Bob Newhart on TV.

"Look at her, Arthur, look at the poor unfortunate; she looks like she's on her last legs. Arthur, we should phone across town to Cecille and see what she's got. Maybe she can put the poor things up. They're all the way from Trudeauland, Arthur."

Arthur kept his eyes glued on Bob Newhart.

I let my eyes roll back a bit to look a bit sicker.

The lady picked up her phone.

"Arthur, maybe Cecille will have something for these poor waifs, look at them, look at her eyes; my god, Arthur, we can't let visitors to Saskatoon ... Hello, Cecille ... Cecille, we have some very sick people here, drove from Ottawa in one day flat and they can't drive another inch ... and they're lovely people from Trudeauland ... very sick ... no, they're not rollers, dear, they're just ordinary ill people from the east who need ... you have ... great! God in Heaven, she's got a cancellation ... did you hear Arthur ... we've saved them! We've got them a place with Cecille."

Arthur was watching the commercial where the

wife rubs the husband's back.

We got directions and got in the car while the lady yelled at Arthur to say goodbye.

He didn't answer.

"Being sick comes in handy," Ryan said when we were inside Cecille's Motel on a busy street in Saskatoon.

I was hungry. Cecille let us use the bar-b-q in the yard and Dad cooked a big steak that he'd bought in Wadena.

That was the best meal I've ever had in my life. Steak with mushrooms and lots of blood on the steak and crispy fat around the outside and big slops of butter all over the baked potato running all over the tinfoil and grease and blood running down your chin and you're wiping your fingers on your shorts and are you ever glad you're alive!

I tried to kiss Ryan with my greasy mouth and we started chasing each other a bit and got sweaty as pigs and then we had a cool bath and went to bed.

There were two Gideon Bibles in the room. I read Ryan the part about a boy named John Nicholson, who was thirteen, who promised his mother that he would read the Bible every day for seventy-three years.

Imagine living for seventy-three years!

Ryan said he was going to live forever. I looked at Dad and he had a funny look on his face. It wasn't sad and it wasn't happy either.

7

It was before six and we were on our way to a picnic ground on the North Saskatchewan River.

We got there in time to see our friend the train cross the river over a big bridge made of black iron. The sun was chasing little piles of mist around and the campers were just getting up and you could smell bacon sizzling. It smelt terrific and it looked terrific.

We had breakfast and then lined up at the public toilets. Mum and I went into the women's while Ryan and Dad waited outside. There was only one door to the women's but when we got inside there were two toilets. A lady with a big sunhat was just going in the second toilet as Mum went in the first.

Then I heard Dad outside say, "PEEEEEEK-A-BOOOO!" in a real silly voice. Then I heard the lady in the sunhat scream.

Soon she stormed out of the toilet. I went out too and Mum came out wondering what was going on.

Dad was outside explaining to the lady and Ryan was hiding behind some bushes.

Dad's face was really red and the lady was storming away in her frilly hat talking to herself.

"I thought that was Mum in there" Dad said,

"and I was just making a joke. I didn't know there were two two toilets in there! She called *me* a peeping tom!"

We left there in a hurry. And everybody laughed for about ten miles down the road.

Except me.

I wanted to go home worse than ever.

8

We were driving the "Yellowhead". The Yellowhead is the highway that follows the route of a half-breed trader of olden times who was called Tête Jaune and everybody knew him because you don't see too many blond Indians. He was murdered but I don't know whether it was because of his hair or not.

That old blond Indian sure walked a long way to get murdered.

Ryan was studying the trains. We were still thinking of the train as being our friend because of the way we were travelling together.

"That's a tender. That's a flatcar. That's a hopper. That's a cattle car. That's a piggy back. That's a refrigerator car. That's a tank car. That's a box car. That's a caboose."

Ryan knows everything there is to know about trains. He got us so interested in trains that when we got to North Battleford we bought eight train hats; four for us and four for our friends in Edmonton who we were going to visit for a few days.

We bought some Saskatchewan bread in North Battleford. Saskatchewan bread is the best bread in the world. It tastes better than cake.

Is Alberta different from Saskatchewan? Yes. Alberta's full of oil. Saskatchewan's full of wheat.

Can you tell when you're in Alberta right away? Sure. Soon as you cross the border, you start to see oil. Immediately.

We drove over the border at Lloydminster. What province is Lloydminster in? Ask the man at the gas station. He doesn't know. How long has he lived in Lloydminster? All of his life. And he doesn't know what province he lives in?

Nope.

Sure enough. Soon as we crossed the border we started seeing the oil. Not gradually. Immediately. It was all over the place.

My uncle has a knick-knack on his bar in his basement that looks like a funny bird. There's water in a little cup and the bird dips his beak in the cup every minute or so.

In the fields and in the backyards in Alberta the oil wells look like my uncle's bird. They dip their beaks into the ground all day and all night long.

After a quick picnic on another river called Vermillion I could tell Dad was getting a little frantic. He wanted to get to Edmonton and have a rest. We'd been in the car for almost a week.

Ryan and I read comics until we got on the hot freeway going to Edmonton. At least, I pretended to read comics; actually I was thinking. Dad was singing with his railway hat on but I knew he didn't really mean it. He was trying to cheer himself up.

He couldn't fool me. He was probably having as rotten a time as I was.

Dad was betting that our friends would say things like this to us when we got there:

"My, have the kids ever grown. Let me look at you, my girl. Look how tall you've become. And Ryan! What a big boy you are. The last time I saw you you were lying in a little wee crib with diapers and everything!"

"Oh no!" Ryan said. He hates it when people talk about when he was a baby and used to wet his pants and everything.

"Remember when Mum took you on the train to Toronto that time and you dirtied your pants and you were smearing peanut butter and stuff all over the seats and all over the windows of the train?"

"Dad!"

Finally, we parked in the back lane behind our friends' house in Edmonton and walked into their backyard. The sprinkler was on and Ryan walked slowly over and stood in the spray. We had driven 325 miles that day and we felt like it. Our legs were stiff and we were sticky and crabby.

Then this human wheel came rolling from around the side of the house. A human girl wheel. Head, legs, hands; head, legs, hands! Rolling right through the sprinkler right to the corner of the big yard, and right around the hedge, counting out loud the whole time.

" ... eighteen, nineteen, twenty ... "

And then rolling towards us.

"Twenty-seven, twenty-eight, twenty-nine ... "

And then right up to where we were standing, she

landed in a perfect Canadian split.

"I have a brother for him!" she said and pointed to Ryan as if he were a lump of dog dirt. "Can you do a back bend?" she said to me.

Then around the corner of the house came a running boy, catching a football. He caught the football, then threw himself a pass, then ran through the sprinkler and caught the pass.

Then he put the ball on the ground, put his hands on his knees, counted "hup one, hup two, hup three," and picked up the ball, rolled on the wet grass, got up, ran right at Ryan, pushed him over with one hand, dodged around him, ran to the hedge, drove the ball into the ground, and put both arms in the air and started cheering.

Then his mother said to me, "My how you have grown! Why the last time I saw you, you were lying in a little wee crib sucking your thumb and dribbling all over the place!"

Then there was Ryan on the ground. He was cackling and laughing and choking and rolling around.

And I was blushing and planning revenge.

I couldn't take this anymore. I was tired of being made a fool of.

Then it was bedtime in Edmonton and I was sleeping with my new friend who thought she was a human girl-wheel and she was talking.

She was talking about round-offs and balance-beams and handstands and walk-overs and dismounts and beating boys on the head with bats and hockey sticks and her mouth was on the wrong end of her face because she was standing on her head at the end of the bed talking to me about swimming and diving while I was tucked in the frilly sheet up to my neck and I had one eye open because the other one was already shut because I was so tired.

And downstairs they were talking about both families going to the Miette Hot Springs.

You don't get much sleep in Edmonton in August.

In Edmonton in August it's never dark for very long. The sun hangs around for all kinds of hours, then goes down for just a little while and then comes right back stronger than ever.

And another thing is this: they don't seem to have any clouds.

Even though their mother kept saying it was the first nice weather they'd had in Edmonton for ten years, I couldn't believe that clouds were even allowed on the premises.

In fact, only one cloud, about the size of my hand, came on the second day we were there, and seemed like such an unwelcome guest that Dad threw an empty beer bottle at it and it went away. That happened at the country club. And it was at that moment, too, that I formulated my run-away plan.

Our friends drove us all out to a fancy country club on a high mountain looking down over the Saskatchewan River.

At about four o'clock in the afternoon the lifeguard blew his whistle and ordered all kids under fourteen out of the pool because it was time that the *adults* had the pool all to themselves. There were about one thousand of us kids under fourteen and about ten adults.

Here we were, supposed to clear out for an hour, and stuck there, all sitting around the pool on towels and benches and hot things grumbling and complaining about equality. Most of the adults were too lazy to swim anyway so there were about three of them dog paddling around and hundreds of us kids sitting there frowning and sweating.

Then Dad got up on the diving board and started yelling out this speech:

"All kids! Listen to this. I'm glad you have to sit it out in the sweaty old sun. I'm glad you have to sit on your bums on the hot places and watch us adults cooling off if we feel like it. You kids have too many privileges. Anybody under fourteen is just a nobody! Why don't you grow up if you want to swim in the cool pool! I say to you this! Kids turn me off! You don't *know* anything! You can't *do* anything! Not like us adults. We're smart. We're better looking. We're bigger than you. We're better swimmers. Adults rule the world. Adults! Adults are kings. Kids are just slaves! Kids are just like ants under our feet. You are a bunch of nothings! Zeros. You don't count. You do what *we* say! At all times. Hurrah for adults and boo on kids under fourteen! Boo! Boo! And again I say Boo!"

Then he jumped off the board and stuck his thumbs in his ears and wiggled his fingers and stuck his tongue out about a foot at all of us.

I was mortified.

That was all everybody needed.

Dozens of kids hit the water the same time he did. Then dozens more piled in after them.

The lifeguard tried to stop them but they just ran right over him.

Dad had caused a revolt.

Just Dad and millions of kids all pushing him under and laughing and chasing him and jumping on his back.

When he finally got to the shallow end he stood up and pointed to the sky.

I was hiding behind my towel.

"Look!" he shouted.

Everybody looked.

It was a small cloud. One tiny cloud the size of my hand.

Dad was out of the pool marching around, chanting:

> A *cloud*, a *cloud*
> It's not a-llowed!
> A *cloud*, a *cloud*
> It's not allowed!"

Then he stopped and put his hand up.

Everybody stopped.

Then he picked up an empty beer bottle from a table and blew across the top of it to start it whistling.

Then he leaned back and threw the bottle at the cloud.

It went whistling up and sailed so high we all

shaded our eyes from the sun.

It fell in a big arc over the fence of the fancy country club and down, down, into the bushes in the valley of the Saskatchewan River without a sound.

Everybody cheered and jumped back in the pool.

Except me.

And everybody laughed.

I didn't.

Dad went and lay down on the grass beside Mum to get his breath.

For the rest of the day, everybody was asking me if that was my Dad.

What I did mostly was cry.

I was so ashamed of my Dad. All the other grownups just sit around quietly and do what they're supposed to, but my Dad always makes a scene. You can always pick him out wherever we go. And this scene was the worst of all.

I hated it when all the kids thought he was so terrific and so much fun and wasn't I lucky to have such a great Dad who does such great things. Oh sure! Really great! I just wanted a Dad like everyone else's.

I wished I could stop crying.

And I wished those kids would forget who my Dad was. And I wished we'd go home!

9

On the way home Mum and Dad were talking about the next day's trip to Miette Hot Springs.

Both families were going.

We were going in both cars.

It was about a two and one-half hour drive to the Springs from Edmonton.

There was some talk of the kids switching cars and being chummy for this part of the trip.

That's when I got my idea.

The next morning after breakfast the scurrying started. Both families were rushing around getting ready.

I sat on the verandah being uncooperative.

I was watching the boy next door polishing his motorcycle. He was tall with beautiful stomach muscles. The sun was shining off the helmet strapped to the back. He was going on a trip, you could tell.

I was imagining going with him when Dad asked me from in the house to help Mum pack the suitcases.

I didn't answer him.

I kept on imagining I was taking off with the boy next door on his motorcycle.

Then I heard Dad say to Mum, "What the hell's the matter with her?"

"There's nothing the matter with *her*," I said through the screen door.

Then Dad burst out the door and his apple was going up and down.

"Get ready," he said very quietly. "We're going to the Miette Hot Springs."

"I'm hot enough. I don't want to go to any Hot Springs."

"Look!" He was shouting now. "All you've done is complain ever since we left Ottawa! Now, one more word out of you and I'm going to hit you one!"

I was staring at him and my lip was starting to curl.

"And don't curl your lip at me, young lady. If you don't like it here with us, why the hell don't you go home?"

Then he went in and slammed the screen door.

Go home. That fit my plan perfectly.

And so did something else.

Our car was parked at the side of the house against their garage. Their car was on the street in front of the house. One couldn't see the other. The garage was in between.

I'd get invited to go in the other car to keep my cartwheel friend company and at the last minute I'd tell them that my Dad wouldn't let me go with them and go back towards our car. I'd duck in the garage and they'd both take off without me.

I went and packed my small suitcase with the flowers on it.

Then I got talking to the cartwheel's Mum about room in their car (they had one of those huge wagons) and she asked me if I'd like to drive as far as the Springs with them. I said that would be really nice if it wasn't too much trouble. Then she asked if maybe her athlete son would like to go in our car with Ryan and he piped up and said he'd rather not because he wanted to work his Dad's CB radio in their own car and I was saved by a 10-4!

Then just when everybody was packed and ready to go I told Dad in my sweetest tone that I'd be going with my friend.

"OK," Dad said, "but hurry, we're leaving right now!"

I said goodbye and ducked around the garage with my suitcase.

Dad and Mum and Ryan said goodbye as I disappeared behind the garage and I heard our motor start.

I rushed over to the other car and told cartwheel's Dad that my Dad wanted me in our car because he wanted to talk to me. He said OK in an understanding way that showed he'd heard the fight Dad and I had had.

"OK," I said. "Dad's all ready to pull out. Just give him the horn!"

I dashed back toward our car but stayed out of view behind the garage with my suitcase and waited.

The second motor started.

Cartwheel's Dad blew his horn the way you rap on doors, da da-da-da-da *da da*! and both cars pulled out slowly and down the street and away.

It worked! By the time they'd find out I'd be on my way home. What a brilliant scheme!

I walked out from behind the garage and looked up at the sky. There was only one little cloud the size of my hand up there in that big, big lonesome Edmonton sky!

And then, I don't have to tell you, I *panicked*!

I ran out on the front lawn and looked frantically up and down the street. It was deserted.

The only things moving were the lawn sprinklers. I was thinking about the map on the ceiling of our car and how long one inch was on that map. And I guess I was crying when I decided I'd have to walk back to Ottawa and I started across the lawn to go down the street in the direction the cars went with my little flowered suitcase and I guess I was quite a pitiful sight.

"Hey, where ya goin'?"

It was the boy next door. It was him with the beautiful stomach muscles and the shiny helmet strapped to the back of his bike.

Hey, where are you going? What a question!

Next thing I knew I was babbling everything that happened in a way that I'm sure he thought was really childish and stupid.

"I'm getting ready to go up to Jasper. I'm leavin' in about ten minutes. We could catch up to them before they get to the Springs."

He went back in the house and came out with a helmet and a leather jacket. He put the helmet on my head and tied my suitcase on the back of his bike.

He showed me how to sit and how to hang on.

We took off down the street and out of Edmonton

at about a thousand miles an hour! The highway with the yellow numbers was still the route. I was still on the trail of old Yellow Head, the old blond Indian, heading for the Rockies. The yellow numbers on the map went way back into Manitoba. What a long way he travelled, old Yellow Head. Old Tête Jaune. He walked and paddled his canoe the whole way more than one hundred and fifty years ago. No roads. No cabins. No Colonel Sanders. No picnic tables. No A & P. No motorcycles. Did he sleep along here where this road was now? Did he have long blond hair and a leather band around his forehead? Tête Jaune, the Iroquois. Murdered on the other side of the Rocky Mountains. Did his wife and children scream in the night when the attackers came to their camp and started to stab them? Did Tête Jaune fight for his life and try to protect his family?

I could feel the boy's muscles through his leather jacket. I hung on as tight as I could. It felt nice holding on like that.

Canada is a huge scary country sometimes.

The road was starting to go up and down.

"Look! Look at the big black clouds. There's a big storm up ahead!" I was yelling in the boy next door's ear.

No answer.

Sure enough, there in the distance, the whole horizon was filled with solid, dark clouds with jagged tops and black bottoms. It was going to be a storm alright.

I looked some more. They were mountains! I

couldn't believe my eyes!

Tête Jaune, did you walk and paddle all this way and then face this? What did you think, Tête Jaune, of these monsters?

No answer.

By the time we got to Hinton the mountains were sitting there ahead of us, like a big wall.

We hadn't said a word to each other for almost an hour. Just him driving and me holding his muscles.

Then I saw the two cars parked outside the restaurant in Hinton. And people standing around. I could see Dad.

I could see Dad, even from that distance. I knew the way he stood. His shirt. I would have recognized him a thousand miles away. The way his head leans a little to the side. The way his shoulders sit.

I could feel love in my stomach.

"Wait. That was them! The two cars parked outside the restaurant. Wait! Stop! Turn around! Yes! That's them! Look at them. They're standing around outside the restaurant. They're talking about me! They can't figure out where I am! I feel so stupid! I wish I was dead! Oh don't! Don't stop! Turn around again! Oh no . . . "

He pulled right up in the middle of them and stopped.

I got off and took off the helmet and jacket. I was shaking.

Everybody was saying my name.

The boy next door gave me my suitcase with the flowers on it.

"Oh Dad," I said. "I ran away!"

The boy next door started his motor and gave everybody a big grin.

"See ya!" he said, and roared off.

I was standing there like Anne does, when she gets off the train at Green Gables. That's what I'd become. A picture off the cover of a book.

Then I said something really brilliant. Dad was walking over to me. He looked like he was going to cry.

"Hey, Dad!" I said.

Imagine. *Hey, Dad.* What a brilliant remark.

Then Dad put his arms around me and gathered me right inside. He was whispering stuff in my ear. Stuff like "Everything's alright now" and "Are you alright?" and "It's OK now, it's OK."

And I had no breath at all to say anything. And that was lucky. Because I might have said something really brilliant again. Something like "Hey, Dad!" or "Lovely weather we're having!"

And then what took place was what my family later came to call the parking lot discussion. We stood in the parking lot outside the restaurant in Hinton, eight of us, two families, and discussed things.

Me, mostly.

How did I get there. The motorcycle. How did I fool everybody. When did I decide. Where did I go. What would have happened if ... Who was the boy. What time did I leave ...

We discussed everything. All at once.

Everything except why.

It puzzled me then.

It doesn't puzzle me now. I know now why they didn't ask why. It was love that made them not ask why.

But then I couldn't figure it out.

All I knew was that I felt *good*!

Then, all of a sudden, our friends decided to go ahead on their trip — they were going to skip lunch for now, skip the Miette Hot Springs — in fact they were going to take off right now and it was very nice to see us and in no time they were gone.

They'd had enough of us, that was for sure.

And I couldn't get Dad's face out of my mind. Dad's face in the parking lot. He looked like he was going to cry.

10

We went into the restaurant and dropped the subject of me.

From the restaurant window I saw a man outside who made my heart stop beating for about an hour. He was walking by the restaurant window. He had on big cowboy boots, jeans and a jacket with leather fringes hanging. There was a string of teeth around his neck. His face was big and handsome with strong bones in his cheeks and a square jaw. His skin was dark reddish brown and he carried a knapsack.

His hair was long and yellow and held out of his eyes with a leather band.

The restaurant door opened and he stepped inside.

He sat at the table next to ours and leaned over to put his knapsack on the floor. When his eyes came up from the floor they looked right at mine. His eyes were wide apart and deep. He froze me to my chair. I tried to look away but I couldn't.

"Tête Jaune," I whispered to Dad across the table without moving my eyes.

The waiter came over to his table and started talking to Yellow Head. The waiter was really rude.

He wanted to see his money before he would let him order his food. Yellow Head spoke in a low, rumbling voice. Why did he have to show his money, he wanted to know. Nobody else did. The waiter put his hands up in the air and said it wasn't *his* fault. It was the rules. He didn't make the rules. Yellow Head rumbled something else. Outside, the mountains were looking blacker and blacker. Yellow Head wasn't going to show his money. He wanted to be served. The waiter said Yellow Head would have to leave.

There was a long quiet.

Then Dad called the waiter over.

"If the guy sits with us, will he have to show his money?"

"I guess not. But you're just going to cause trouble."

Dad got up and went over to Yellow Head's table. There was a low conversation. Then they both came back to our table and sat down. Dad started talking.

"Are the mountains bigger than they look from here?"

"Do they look big to you?" asked Yellow Head.

"I think so. This is our first time here so I have no way of telling."

"They sure look big to me," I said.

"Me too," Ryan said.

Yellow Head made a sort of speech, looking at me the whole time.

"If they seem big to you from here, they won't seem as big when you get there. Everything is different than it looks to be. The lakes that seem big and deep are small and shallow. The lakes that look small and shallow are big and deep. The land that looks kind is cruel. The sky that looks fierce is friendly."

We ate slowly to let him catch up and when we were finished Dad picked up our check and left Yellow Head's on the table.

We all looked at Dad. Wasn't he going to pay for Yellow Head's meal?

Then Yellow Head picked up his check and we all went to the cash register.

Dad paid for ours.

The waiter looked nervous.

Big Yellow Head paid and while he waited for his change he reached into the bowl of mints on the counter and took a big fistful and shoved them into his pocket. I noticed some of his teeth were bad in front.

"Need a lot of these," Yellow Head said to the waiter. "Kills the taste of the food you serve here."

"Indian," the waiter mumbled as though he called him a dirty name.

"No," said Yellow Head, "Iroquois."

"What's the difference?"

"Big difference. 'Indian' is a white man's word."

We left the restaurant and Yellow Head waved goodbye and walked down the road toward the mountains. Then he cut down a side road and disappeared behind some trees.

Another person I'd never, never see again!

11

As we moved closer to the mountains, I thought of the blood one hundred and fifty years ago, the stabbing and the screams on the other side of the rocks that were as high as clouds.

Yellow Head was right. The first mountain didn't look as high when we stopped the car and walked around the rocks beside the road. From a distance the broken rocks at the bottom of the mountain looked small and the mountain looked big. When we got up close, the rocks at the bottom were huge, as big as our house in Ottawa, and the mountain looked smaller, like a tall broken building.

I stuck close to Dad while we explored.

But our first Rocky Mountain was only a midget. As we drove further and started to climb and turn, I tried to keep my first mountain in sight. As we moved away from it, I watched it grow. The further we got, the bigger it got. I nearly turned around to tell Ryan to look but didn't because in front of us the same thing was happening and on both sides of us it was happening too. Every mountain was either getting smaller or getting bigger. We were surrounded by growing and shrinking mountains. Getting bigger, getting smaller, getting bigger, getting smaller, breathing in and getting bigger, breathing out and getting smaller, swelling and shrinking, rising and falling, always changing, never looking like what they are — *oh! Tête Jaune*, you know so many secrets!

It was late afternoon when we got to the Miette Hot Springs.

Mum was the first in for a change. No wonder. The water was just like a hot bath at home except it was yellow and smelled a little like hard boiled eggs.

I expected a kind of hot river that we would all go and sit in, but it was a regular swimming pool with dressing rooms, a shallow end, a deep end, deck chairs and all that. The only difference was that you don't really swim, you just wallow around and sigh a lot.

Ryan got a bunch of dirty looks from a group of grannies and grandpas at the deep end when he did a cannonball in the middle of them. Mum stayed the whole time near where the real hot sulphur was pouring in until she was wrinkled up like a golden prune. The sounds there were strange. Usually when there's a pool full of people there's crying and screaming and yelling and laughing and shrieking and people splashing and mothers running after babies and bratty boys stealing towels and fathers throwing their kids up in the air; but in this hot, yellow, egg-smelling water everything was strangely quiet.

Even when people laughed, they laughed without making any noise. They'd just sort of open their mouths and throw their heads back but no sound would come out. And even Ryan was just standing there, up to his chin in the yellow water, staring straight ahead.

I went into the dressing room to cool off and change. I sat on a bench for a long time and stared at a lady wringing out a towel in a hand wringer. I was looking at how pink her kneecaps were when I noticed something strange happening. At first I didn't know what it was. Something was different that's all.

Then I realized. It was sounds. Sounds of shouting and crying coming from the pool.

The lady with the pink kneecaps went to the door of the dressing room and stuck her head out.

"My God. Somebody's dead!" she said and came back and sat down on the bench beside me.

"A man. Must be a heart attack or something."

A man?

I jumped up and ran out the door to the yellow air and the pool. There was a big crowd standing around one end of the pool. There was nobody in the water. I couldn't see Dad anywhere.

I pushed my way in through the hot pink bodies in the crowd until I could see somebody lying on his back on the tile. I tried to see his face but I couldn't.

A man was kneeling beside him hitting him on the chest with his fist.

He was pounding and pounding and I could hear the sound of the pounding, a thumping sound, and my heart was pounding too because I was staring at the bathing suit the lying man was wearing.

It was Dad's bathing suit!

My voice shouted.

"Dad!" was the word that came out.

Then I felt a hand on my shoulder.

"Mum's gone to get changed. We'd better go."

I turned around.

"Dad?"

"Come on. Let's go." He was talking very quietly. I was looking right into Dad's face. I could hear his voice over the pounding on the lying man's chest behind me.

"Dad?"

"Let's get changed," Dad said. He was stroking the back of my neck with his fingers like I was a cat.

"Dad? He has a bathing suit just like yours!" I whispered.

"Come on. Let's just go."

"Dad. The bathing suit. I thought ... "

Dad took me by the hand and trailed me through the crowd to the dressing rooms.

After we got changed and we were leaving I took a quick peek at the lying man. Somebody was putting a big towel over him. His eyes were squeezed shut and his mouth was wide open. His grey hair was lying on the tile a little bit, sort of wet.

And his feet were blue and very sad looking.

I looked at the bathing suits the men were wearing. Quite a few of them looked a bit like Dad's.

There were a lot of stairs from the water down to the parking lot. We walked down in single file, not because the stairs were narrow but because we all wanted to use the railing because we were so weak.

All of us except Ryan. Here we were, our knees wobbly, hanging on the railing. And here he was, running up and down the stairs beside us, talking and laughing and fooling around. He was acting just like one of those dogs that don't get taken out for a drive in the car very often and who take a fit if anybody starts to go anywhere.

I couldn't figure out where he got all the energy. Was it because he was a boy? No. Dad was a boy and right now he looked like he was made out of spaghetti before you put the sauce on. Was it because Ryan was young? I was young and I wasn't going around like a fly caught between windows, specially after being soaked in hot egg water for about an hour!

Later, Dad said maybe the altitude and the sulphur worked on different people in different ways.

It made me delirious.

It made Mum sleepy.

It made Ryan hyper.

And Dad?

"It gives me extra powers to see into the future and foretell what will happen."

"Sure, Dad. What will happen when we get to Jasper?"

"I will sit in our rented cabin, open a can of beer, drink it, and then I will heave a big sigh."

He was right. That's exactly what happened.

By the time the sigh was heaved, Ryan and I were heading down to the banks of the Athabaska River, which flowed right past our cabin.

98

The Athabaska River is wide and shallow and frothy and fast and grey coloured and clean looking. It's a beautiful and exciting river.

And cold. Ask Ryan. He slipped in twice and got the "How am I to get these pants dry by morning?" speech before he went to sleep.

Before I went to sleep, Dad and I sat by the cabin window watching the tiny light of the Sky Tram crawl slowly up and down Whistler's Mountain on its wire. It could have been a "phosphorescent spider" Mum said, going up and down in slow motion building its web.

"We'll go on that tomorrow," Dad said. "Anybody going to be scared?"

"I'll be scared," I said. "I'm scared of heights."

"Stay close to me and you won't be scared," Dad said. "Anyway, millions of people have gone up and nobody's ever been hurt."

"I'm not afraid of anything," Mum said.

I went easily to sleep. The Athabaska River has a deep voice. It hums you to sleep. It never, never takes a breath. Not for years, not for centuries, not for ...

I would ask Mum the next morning what the word for one thousand years is, and then the word for longer than that, much longer than that ...

The Athabaska just never, never, takes a breath.

12

After breakfast Ryan and Mum and I went down to the edge of the Athabaska again and listened to the deep voice.

"Decade is ten years. Century is a hundred years. Millennium is a thousand years. Eon is years and years and ages and ages." I was repeating Mum's lesson in time. And I was trying to stretch my mind so that I could think about how long an eon was. It was how long the Athabaska roared his deep roar. I stretched my mind. I grunted and held my breath and forced my mind to wrap around that long, long time. I thought of the summer and how long it was, and how long ago it was that I was in grade four and how long next year would be and then I thought of myself after Dad and Mum were dead and then after I was an old wrinkled lady and how *that* wouldn't even be a century yet and then my mind kind of popped like a bubble gum bubble and collapsed and for a few minutes I couldn't think of anything.

My mind was blank. Only the Athabaska River roared by.

Later in the line-up for the Sky Tram to go up Whistler's Mountain I was telling Dad about the lump in my stomach.

"Remember," Dad was saying, "things don't usually turn out the way they *look* like they're going to turn out."

"That's what the Indian said," I said.

"I'm petrified," Mum said.

"Look at the neat machinery," Ryan said.

There are two sky trams. One is at the top of the mountain, loading up with people coming down, and one at the bottom loading up with crazies like us who want to go up.

We got on the tram. You stand and hang on to bars or straps. A girl in a uniform showed us where to stand. There was a sign on the wall saying something about thirty people being allowed on at a time.

I was counting the people as they got on. Every time a person got on, the tram would sink a bit as though we were hanging there by an elastic. Twenty-six. Sink a bit. Twenty-seven. Sink a bit more. Twenty-eight. Twenty-nine. No more. Enough. We'll never make it up on the mountain. Please don't let any more on!

Then the fattest, happiest man I ever saw came puffing up. Right this way. Oh no! He stepped on, laughing and joking about the cable breaking and stuff.

We sank about a foot and bounced for a while.

The girl in the uniform closed the doors and in this bored voice started to tell us about the trip and how many accidents they'd never had and how big the cable was and how many feet we were going to climb.

Then we started, very slowly.

101

I imagined the guy at the top turning the crank, grunting, looking at his watch, hating his job, deciding to go to lunch or just quitting in the middle and letting us go crashing back down in a mess of laughing adults and screaming kids.

"Don't be scared," Dad said.

Soon we were going much faster and smoother and I started to feel a lot better because everything seemed lighter and easier now that we were up so high.

I was actually enjoying it by the time we were half way up and passing the other tram coming down.

I looked up at Dad.

His eyes looked like two devilled eggs and he was hanging on to the bar with both hands. His ears were red and his cheeks were white. His teeth were clamped together and his lips were apart. He looked like somebody on the Bugs Bunny Hour who was being electrocuted.

I put my arm around his waist.

"Don't be scared, Dad. We'll be off in a minute."

"Takes eons," Dad said between his teeth.

The little town of Jasper was below us. It could have been made of Lego blocks.

The mountains and lakes stretched away as far as I could see.

It was easy to imagine all this being like this for a century. My mind was even stretching to a millennium. The Athabaska was lying down there, between the mountains, like a silver Christmas tree icicle on its side.

We got off and walked around the top for a while. Dad was looking better, although he said his knees felt wobbly.

The air was cold as though somebody had a fridge door open somewhere.

A few tiny snowflakes floated by, did little tricks and floated over the edge of Whistler's Mountain. They didn't need to go down by the sky tram.

It was all so peaceful.

That is, until we noticed Ryan.

Ryan, my only brother, was a short distance off, near the edge, chasing a snowflake!

Dad let a roar out of him that would have broken all the government windows in Ottawa.

Ryan turned suddenly towards us and tripped and fell on his side and skidded on the rock and mossy mountain flowers. He was about ten feet from the edge.

Dad was half way to him by the time Ryan stopped skidding.

Dad stumbled and went down on one knee and bounced right up again.

By the time Mum and I arrived they were both half sitting together on the rock. Ryan was crying. Dad had that look on his face that I saw in the motel in Saskatoon when Ryan said he was going to live forever.

Later, all the way down in the tram, Dad had his arm around Ryan hugging him close.

I wasn't jealous.

I was thinking, on the way down, how long it takes

to go down Whistler's Mountain.

The snowflake, about a half an hour; the tram about five minutes; Ryan would take less than a minute.

Later that afternoon I saw something fall from another mountain that made me think about time in a new way.

We were standing at the bottom of Mount Edith Cavell looking at the Angel Glacier. We drove a long winding steep road and walked for about an hour to get there. Dad carried Ryan part way because his thigh had a big deep scrape on it and he was limping.

Near the top of the mountain is a chunk of ice miles wide and miles high and miles deep shaped like a peaceful angel with her wings spread out. I was looking at the wings of the angel when I noticed a kind of small bunch of snowflakes floating off the tip of one of her wings. It looked so strange to see a little snowstorm like that, so far away, on such a sunny day. Then I heard a crack, like a gun or quick thunder, and then a huge booming rolling echoing roar that got so loud it seemed to shake the whole mountain and us too. As the flakes floated down they got bigger and started bouncing, like in slow motion on TV. The further down Mount Edith Cavell they came, the bigger they got. And then, more noise like cracking wood started echoing up and down the valley. When the flakes hit the bottom in front of us they were as big as houses! They were rolling over each other and smashing and crashing and crushing around, these huge pieces of ice, sending chunks away up in the air like an explosion.

We just stood there with our mouths open.

Nothing is what you think it is!

A snowfall turns out to be tons of huge blocks of ice.

An angel isn't peaceful at all.

You could die chasing a snowflake.

How long did it take for the ice to fall? Less than a minute! How long was all this going on? An eon!

They were the same. A minute. An eon!

It seemed we were watching that ice fall forever. But it was only a few seconds. Right now, I am still watching Ryan chase that snowflake. He will chase it as long as I think about it. I could change a few seconds into years!

I was so excited I couldn't talk.

That night, snuggled in bed in our cabin in Jasper, I watched Dad put a new bandage on his knee and listened to Mum wind our clock. Poor clock. So pitiful to be a clock when you're around rivers, mountains and glaciers like these.

I went to sleep listening to my heart thumping quietly in my ears. My clock and my heart . . .

13

I woke up from a dream.

It was almost dark in my dream, and Dad made a fire about ten feet tall by the side of the lake.

We were all standing around the fire warming our hands because of the cold coming off the big angel.

I could only see everybody's face through the flames and when I turned and looked over the lake, the flames made a pointed red light across the water almost to the other side.

Then, in the light I saw Dad rowing a boat as fast as he could towards us on the shore.

It was only a dream but it was clear as a movie.

Behind him the mountain was black against the dark sky and the glacier was dropping giant boulders of ice into the water. The ice made huge waves as it fell into the water behind Dad's boat and we were yelling and yelling at him to row faster. Faster, Dad, faster!

When I opened my eyes, I saw Dad across the cabin, buttering some toasted buns with jam.

"I'm going as fast as I can," he said, and started slopping jam all over the place, pretending he was in a bun-and-jam race of some kind.

I checked the clock by Mum's bed. It was 6:30 a.m.

One tick of the clock.

I was getting older by the minute!

Later that morning I had almost forgotten about my theories about time when we arrived at the Columbia Ice Fields.

One of the glaciers is the Athabaska Glacier.

Here we are, standing on miles and miles of ice, hundreds of feet thick in the middle of August!

Our tour guide sounded a little like Smokey the Bear.

"Hundreds of millions of years ago, there was a shallow sea here. But internal pressure caused the land to change and where there had been water, mountains rose. Thirty-five million years ago, the earth's crust relaxed ... the ice you are now standing on is flowing like a river. But this river of ice moves only one-fifth of an inch an hour. Why only five hundred years ago, the ice was over there where your cars are parked...."

I couldn't stand any more. I clamped my hands over my ears and started talking to myself.

"One-fifth of an inch an hour! No more. No more. No more time! Please! No more!"

Then we drove and the mountains grew and shrank and grew and shrank and the road went up and down and in and out and we stopped for lunch and started again and the five-hundred-million-year-old mountains stared down at us.

By the time we got to Golden in British Columbia, I felt about the size of a minute.

Thank goodness!

No more time problems here.

Just a motel about two feet from a railroad track and a TV set with President Nixon on it all the time and Mum with her ham and cabbage cooking and a little stream where we stuck our feet in and Dad putting a fresh bandage on Ryan's gashed thigh.

Later that night, a train would go by every little while and rattle the whole cabin.

Dad was fooling around bouncing up and down in the bed and pretending he was going to fall out every time a train would go by.

"Is thi-s ev-er a peace - ful qui - et - place to ha - ve - a rest - af - ter - a - long - drive - through the - five - hun - dred - million - year - old mount - ains!" he would say while the train rumbled by and he was bouncing up and down on the bed as if there was an earthquake.

We laughed a lot and then went to sleep.

It was my turn to make Dad feel good and I was trying to figure out how to do it.

After breakfast with our friend the train going by all the time and after Ryan got Dad's arms and legs and head sockets put back in place because of all the shaking he said he went through during the night and after Mum cut up the rest of the ham and made sandwiches for our lunch and after Dad drove out to get some ice for the cooler and after everything was finally cleaned up and packed and ready to go, I got up.

I pretended I was asleep a lot longer than I really was and just spent the time listening to the family talking and bustling around while I tried to find cool places on the pillow for my face and cool crannies in the sheets to stick my feet. And while I tried to think.

Then I sat up and stretched like a big queen and pretended I didn't realize how much I had been goofing off. I'm a real phony sometimes.

Of course Dad made a big fuss about sleepy heads and all that and Mum said, "How convenient for her" and Ryan watched the trains shunting by the cabin window.

It was hazy and hot when we stopped right smack in the centre of Roger's Pass, a huge green misty valley in the middle of the Selkirk Mountains.

"If they hadn't found this pass when they did Canada might belong to the United States right now," Dad said.

"How educational!" Ryan said.

Dad ignored him and went right ahead.

"They wanted to join the oceans by train line so that Canada would make sense from Atlantic to Pacific."

"*A mari usque ad mare*," Mum said, pulling off one of her better ones.

"What?" said Ryan.

Later when we stopped for a sandwich at a picnic table at Craigellachie I read on a sign that here the last spike was hammered in the railroad and that did it from sea to sea. A man named Smith took a whack in 1885 and bent the spike over just like I do when I'm helping Ryan hammer one of his forts at home. They let Smith try another one and he got it right this time.

"How educational!" Dad said.

At Sicamous we turned down into the Okanagan Valley. It was the start of the hottest afternoon of driving on our whole trip.

Lucky fruit trees getting doused in water from thousands of hoses attached to moving wheels that are almost human the way they walk along the paths!

Stop and look at the floating bridge at Kelowna. Lucky floating bridge at Kelowna. Lucky floating bridge, you look so cool in that sparkling water!

We drive on.

Dad stops at Peachland at the beer store. Peachland! What a refreshing name. The sign says, "Beer On Ice!" Dad is going towards the store. Now he is running. He disappears into the store. Soon he is out again. He is walking slowly. His face is long. He's lost his best friend.

"There's a beer strike!"

No beer in Peachland.

Try Summerland.

We drive to Summerland. Welcome to Summerland! Thousands of square dancers. "It's a Square Dance Convention! Not a room in the valley vacant this week let me tell you!"

"We'll trade our automobile and two healthy intelligent children for twelve bottles of beer, any brand!" Mum says with ice in her voice.

"Sorry. Sent our last beer back out to Peachland. Big yacht race up there. Try Penticton!"

We try Penticton.

Sorry. Best bet is to get out of the valley.

We get out of the valley.

It was sunset when we arrived at Hedley. Ryan and I were lying exhausted in the back. The map on the roof looked like it was going to melt. I looked across at Ryan who was sleeping in the position babies use before they are born. I half closed my eyes and pretended he was a small chicken going around inside one of the chicken ovens in the A & P.

Ryan was looking well-done and Dad was getting worried. We wouldn't survive the night in the car. We were too filthy and stiff and grumpy and sticky and dizzy and hungry and sore and fed up.

Except me. I was enjoying myself and I was plotting.

Dad stopped for gas at a station in the deep forest near Princeton. It was almost dark. Dad asked the gas man what our chances were down the road.

"What's wrong with right here? We got cabins. We got a campsite. We got a nice bar-b-q. We got corn on the cob. We got beer. We got a river. We got a little nice beach. We got nice soft beds. We got everything you want. It's not fancy but we got it. Wanna coffee while you're deciding?"

"But I thought this was only a gas station."

"No No! Out back. We got the works. Just haven't got my new sign on yet. Just gonna turn it on right now. Wanna see the sign?"

"Marrrgerrrie! Turn on the goddam sign, will ya please?"

While the roast chicken and I crawled out of our oven, the sign came on.

111

Golden Dawn.

Back in the trees a bit behind the gas station but big and beautiful!

Beautiful!

Golden Dawn. Golden Dawn! The name is like a bell ringing. The name is like those guys feel who are lost in the desert on the late movie and who finally stagger to a water hole in the sand and stick their faces in for about an hour until they have to pull out and they're all whiskers and filth and kind of crazy the way they are looking around and there's water running down their chins and onto their ripped dirty shirts.

Down behind Golden Dawn, a yappy little river and a place to cook and a place to eat and a beautiful, silly- looking cabin to sleep in.

And a tiny camping ground.

And one little tent on a shady spot beside the yappy little river. And in front of the tent a young couple in love lying down looking up waiting for the stars to come out. And a radio beside them. And on the radio — Roberta! I had almost forgotten about Roberta.

> *That's the time*
> *I feel like makin' love to you . . .*

Good old Roberta.

And good old beautiful Golden Dawn.

I was too tired to float away. I was thinking of millions of things; time and love and a question I was going to ask Dad. A question . . .

The question!

To ask certain questions the time has to be right. You can't just jump up and ask certain types of questions just any old time you feel the urge.

"Not too long after the town of Hope, we get on a freeway into Vancouver. We'll be in the big city by this evening," Mum was saying.

What we saw at Hope made me think of the question again.

Near Hope we drove over what was left of a valley and a place where a pretty little lake had once been. Some skeletons and a few cars are underneath the piles and piles of rock we drove over. The people never knew what hit them. The mountain had fallen on them.

We bought beautiful bread in the Hope bakery and started down the Fraser Delta. We stopped on the side of the highway at a picnic table and had our lunch and looked at the water and the comfy farms below us and the train moving silently along just as peaceful as could be.

A couple came running over to us. I thought Dad and Mum must have known them the way they were saying hello. But then, they didn't know our names so why were they so glad to see us?

Ryan noticed it first. It was their Ontario licence plates. They were from Ontario.

Big deal!

Ontario is as big as Europe, remember? Would a guy from Europe get all excited if he met another guy from Europe?

"He would if they met on Mars or some such remote colony as that," Mum said.

Licence plates don't make me homesick or lonely. Thoughts do. Places like the Hope landslide do.

A whole mountain falls on you. Right out of the blue. All your plans. All the crying and laughing ... Finished. Splatt! A mountain falls on you. You're flatter than your clothes are when you're not in them. There's not even the smell of your pipe tobacco left. You're like all the ghosts at Portage and Main. Dying and loving somebody. I always end up thinking of those two together. Dying and loving.

I was all set to ask the question.

Then Mum said, "At the end of the freeway is Vancouver. In Vancouver there is a Holiday Inn where we will reward ourselves with a luxury evening consisting of a sumptuous meal, wine, expensive surroundings, pool, sauna, colour TV, king-sized beds and room service. And don't forget. Tomorrow is your father's birthday."

Dad's birthday! That was it! I'd wait till then to ask him the question!

We hit the freeway.

Birthdays are the best days for questions.

The question could wait till tomorrow.

A freeway is just a freeway and it passed slowly by and in the early evening we piled out of the car in big downtown Vancouver, Holiday Inn style, with the big green sign with the star on top and the big doorman and big lobby with the big mirror that we stopped and looked at ourselves in. This was the first time we had been with ordinary travellers.

The mirror did not tell us any lies. We looked like we had crawled on our hands and knees all the way from Halifax!

It took us an hour in our huge double room to get the grime off. Dad sent the car to be washed inside and out, Mum sent the clothes down to be washed, Dad ordered before-dinner snacks and gin to be sent up to our room and Mum said we were spending money like drunken sailors.

Down to the dining room. This time we looked OK. Just like ordinary travellers.

The waiter bent over Ryan and me and then talked as though we weren't there.

"Children eat free, sir, from this special menu." Dad started reading the menu in this serious tone to Ryan and me as though we couldn't read it ourselves. He read the whole menu. It was almost like the speech he made in Edmonton from the diving board. Only quieter.

"Hey Dad! Kids eat free! Chica-chica-chicken is fri- fri- fri-fried, two pieces big with Frenchie frenchie fries, roll and butter, milk or Cola-rola. Oodle oodle noodle-ghetti makes it fun to roll it up and wiggle it down the old channel with a delicious meat sauce served with Roly poly roll and Patty-pat butter pat, milk or Cola-rola. Super sizzle whiz-burger, still cracklin' and hot from the super-grill — a super burger for a super appetite served on a bunny bun, relish and picky pickle slices, french fries, milk or Cola-rola. Scoobie doobie bun doggie dog; it won't bark and you'll do the bitin' on this hot grilled dog on a crispy toasted bun with real live relish and pickle slices, potato chippies, milk or Cola-rola. Brought to you by the most accommodating people in the world!"

Fried chicken, spaghetti, hamburg, hotdog. What a menu.

Ryan was laughing so hard his face was getting red because he wasn't making a sound.

Mum and I were looking at the tablecloth.

"And which would the children prefer?" the waiter said.

"The kids'll have two steaks, rare," Dad said.

Later, on Dad's suggestion, we went into the pool on a full stomach. Mum went back to the room to read and plan for tomorrow.

Then we flopped into the big king-sized beds.

Dad was on the outside of one big blue bed and I was on the outside of the other one. We were so far apart we started saying goodnight to each other pretending we were at opposite ends of a huge field.

"Gooooooood Night."

"Gooooooood Niiiiiiiiiiite!"

On the ceiling of our room in the Holiday Inn that night they had fake stars!

The most accommodating people in the world!

"Good Niiiiiiiiiiiiiite!"

14

We were coming to the end.

Mum was organized.

Up at five. The fake stars still shining.

We played "Emergency".

Mum got us out before six. We looked in the big mirror in the lobby. We looked good. We got in our clean car.

At a quarter to seven we drove onto the ferry with a million other cars.

It was question day. Dad's birthday.

Breakfast on the ferry. Ryan was planning his order.

"Hey, Dad! I'm going to have silver dollar flip flop flapjacks, flipped just right and flopped just once, five silver-dollar-sized cakes from the pan with whipped butter, fresh from the Canadian Maple sappy-syrup, milk or hot chocolate on the side."

He was reading from an extra menu on his lap he had taken from the world's most accommodating people.

"What do you want?" Dad said with his eyes closed.

"Pancakes," Ryan said.

Off the ferry at Nanaimo.

By ten in the morning we were shopping in a Port Alberni A & P. Close your eyes a bit and you're in Ottawa in the A & P. Down the street in Port Alberni, there's the cross-eyed Colonel on his bucket of chicken. Close your eyes a bit and you're back home looking at the cross-eyed Colonel.

We're heading towards the Pacific on our last lap.

The hills start again.

We stop and walk into a giant bush. The trees are nine hundred years old the sign says. Mum and Ryan and Dad join hands and hug a tree trunk. The sun comes through the huge branches like golden flashlights. Beams come slanting down with dust in them like they did in church when I used to go.

We drive again.

I'm getting my question sorted out. I'm going to ask about God and Time and Love and Grandpa and the Hope disaster and Eons. And Dad's not going to get out of it. None of his funny wiggly answers.

And I'm going to make him feel good.

We drive again.

Who will see the Pacific first?

Will it be Mum, queen of maps and chief navigator? Will it be Dad, who is checking the mileage thing? "We've driven 3,807 miles." Will it be Ryan? Will it be me?

We start to go down hills.

The air starts to get cooler.

"There! There! Through those trees!" It's Mum who sees it first. "The Pacific! There it is!"

Soon we are driving right along the shore. A sign

says: 49th Parallel — Pacific Rim.

Hundreds of young people lying along the sand.

On your left, ladies and gentlemen, the Pacific Ocean!

Long Beach.

We drive.

We want Tofino. The town of Tofino. Look on the map. It's as far as you can go!

In Tofino there is no A & P. There is no Colonel. There is no Simpson's.

There is Jones' General Store. There is Mrs. Trenholm's Fish Bar. There is Jim's Gas. This is a different world!

We buy two huge crabs from Lottie's Fish Wharf and go to a private part of the beach to have Dad's birthday party.

Ryan is throwing stones at Japan.

Mum is grabbing some sun.

Dad makes a big fire on the sand.

He tears the shells of the crabs.

We eat small carrots, beans, corn on the cob and cold crab.

We are lying around the fire.

It's time for the question.

I have it all figured out. It's about Time and Seconds and Eons and Love and Death and Age.

Dad is speaking. "Well, I'm forty years old today."

Now! Do it now!

"Hey, Dad! Are you going to die?"

No! No! That's not it. That's not what I want to know! It came out all wrong! No! No! My bottom lip is starting to shake up and down. He's going to think I'm a terrible idiot. What a thing to ask somebody on their birthday!

But wait. What did he say? What's that he said? Did I hear him right? He just nodded and said, "Oh sure!" Now I am crying because he's going to die and I guess I am also crying because I'm so dumb to ask such a dumb question! He's got his arms around me. He's patting me on the back. There, there.

"And I'll tell you what," he is saying with that serious tone, "I'll cut down on my smoking so I won't cough too much at your wedding and embarrass you."

"Hey, Dad! Come and dive into the waves!" Ryan says and takes off.

"OK," Dad says and takes my hand.

"You know," he says, "a few months before your Grandpa died when he was over at our place and I was putting in that stone walk in our back yard he did something that I thought was really smart. He was standing around watching me when all of a sudden he got down on his knees and wanted to put one of the stones in himself. He worked on it for about fifteen minutes fitting it and making sure it was level and packed right and permanent. Then he stood up and told me that every time I used that walk from now on I'd see that stone and think of him. He was right. Even though he's dead, every time I go down that walk I can feel him there. He was right. He beat time all to hell that way."

Our feet were in the Pacific.

We waded in a little deeper.

Ryan and Mum were watching us.

The water was up over the top of my bathing suit.

I put my arms around his neck and wrapped my legs around his stomach. I put my lips against his ear. His curly hair was tickling my nose.

"Now *this* is educational," I said.

His arms tightened around me and stayed that way for a long time.

This was as far west as we could go.

I can still feel his curly hair tickling my nose and the waves rocking us back and forward.

And it seems like only a second ago.